I0716674

Travis I. Sivart

THE T.A.L.O.N. AGENCY

Travis I. Sivart

Travis I. Sivart

The T.A.L.O.N. Agency

Copyright © 2018 Travis I. Sivart

Book Cover Art and Design by Melody Hasselvander of RagdollComics.com

Edited by Tara Moeller

Talk of the Tavern Publishing Group

Travis I. Sivart

Love Sci-Fi, fantasy, and a story that arcs across worlds?
Grab a free eBook at

TravisISivart.com/FreeBook

DEDICATION

To those who have inspired me to strive for more, by their words, needs, actions, love, or respect. Andrea and Aidan stand out above all others. You're my down and dirty, nitty-gritty, street-level superheroes.

Contents

CASE 1669
CODENAME: SMOKE AND CINDER

Hector Rodriguez crouched in bushes on the side of a hill, his antiquated Bushmaster ACR DMR at the ready. It had been top of the line well over a decade ago, but with all the modifications, it was still better than anything else out there. Thoughts ticked through his head like the beats of a tune from his younger years. It was hard to keep track when he was hunting. One hunt blended with the next, losing names of people and places. He shook his head, trying to lose the thought of why he bothered at all. He knew why. He remembered the faces of cold corpses of the team he had built, and his partner, Paulina, on the day he walked away from T.A.L.O.N. They had taken something from him, and now he would take from them. They hunted him, and now he hunted them.

Calling upon his training from ten years in the Marine Corps, Hector dropped to his belly and crawled forward in the wet grass and the predawn light. The smell of sod and gun oil drifted across his awareness. The yellow lenses of his shooter's glasses clicked to life with the heads up display transmitted from his weapon. The readouts on the weapon itself would not be seen by anyone without glasses set to the right frequency, and then only if they were within three feet. If anyone got that close, they would already be dead.

Rising onto his elbows, Hector saw that one sentry stood on duty, the man's silhouette flaring behind him as he flicked a lighter to life to light his cigar, leaning forward and cupping it.

Now, while the man was night blind from the flame, Hector

struck.

A shot rang out and the man collapsed. There was no muting the noise, even with a suppressor, in this brick and cinder-block canyon between the warehouses. Hector waited to see if anyone else was close enough or awake enough to have heard the echoing retort of his rifle. Dropping to his belly and settling the barrel of his weapon on his knife – which he had jammed into the soil – he settled down to wait one hundred and eighty seconds. When he had counted to forty, lights came on in the upper level. By ninety-two, lights blossomed in the lower floor. At one hundred thirty-six, he set his eye to his scope and waited for the door to open.

When it did, three men came out, waving their 9mm guns at the night. One stumbled over the foot of their friend who lay dead to one side of the door.

"Idiots," Hector thought, "didn't check corners, or even bother to look down. Fucking amateurs."

He took sight of the man looking down, his head centered in the crosshairs and squeezed the trigger. The rifle popped and snapped up, and the man dropped onto his friend. Hector fired three more quick shots on semi-auto, leaving a tight cluster of holes in the shoulder, neck, and throat of another of the men. Pivoting the weapon the slightest amount, he put a slug into the ass of the third man who was trying to run back inside. The man fell inside the door, his legs holding it open.

Hector waited to see exactly how stupid the man would be. Luck was with the hunter tonight; the hunted was a moron. Instead of pulling his legs in and crawling around a corner, the man sat up to pull his legs in, and reached for the door knob to close the door. Another shot, and the man's hand went limp on the handle, his body slumping to the ground with a bullet in his head.

That would be the night shift taken care of; now to get the boss before the morning shift arrived.

Hector pulled his bayonet from the dirt and wiped it on his sleeve, then clipped it to the end of his modified suppressor. Crouching low, becoming as small a target as possible, he covered the ground between the bushes and the building.

Stopping at the four dead men, he picked up the cigar and looked at the band. "Decent stick," he muttered, and popped it in his mouth. Focusing on the tip, Hector used his gifts, and the cigar began to smolder. Smoke curled away from the end of the cigar. The man drew in deep and blew smoke inside the door held open by the dead man's legs.

The smoke continued to billow forth, embers mixing with the smoldering cloud as dust and airborne particles ignited, filling the room beyond the door. Flowing and moving like a thing alive, it grew and expanded.

Hector backed away, around the corner, and knelt. Settling the stock of his rifle against his shoulder, he waited for his real quarry to come out.

In less than a minute, the sound of coughing and footsteps came towards him.

Hector walked away from the police station, folding the check and tucking it into his shirt pocket. Eight years as a cop, He'd learned how to turn in a prisoner without being held up by red tape, and how long to stay for them to figure out who he really was. Having a front business - and Paulina there to cover it - as a bondsman allowed him to get jobs to fund his real work. It also helped that good men like Rich, a local beat cop, and Alex, a Federal Marshal, still worked with him and were willing to lend a hand, making sure things went smooth.

Good men like them made the job worth it. Hector knew he could do things and go places that uniformed officers never could, at least not legally. And helping them clean the streets was always worth it.

Swinging a leg over his hog, he straddled the bike. Looking in one of the mirrors, he ran his fingers through his beard, then his hair, noting the silver wings above his ears, in his sideburns, and on his chin, contrasting with the ebony of the rest of his hair. Was he really that old, or was it the stress of being a bounty hunter on the run from the law that did it?

He fit his helmet over his head and buckled it on. Without thinking, he flicked the foot control and started the bike. Shifting down, he pulled into traffic, flicking the pedal up to shift gears and zoom away with the growl of the engine echoing off the stone buildings. It was early, but it was time for a drink.

Otherwise he would get busy thinking.

Jack looked up from his table when the door of Los Portales Oscuros Cigar Bar opened, letting in the blinding light of the sun, dust motes dancing and the smell of cars and morning filling the room. A silhouette filled the doorway a moment later and the door slowly drifted closed behind Hector. Touching the brim of his fedora, Jack nodded, and raised his rock tumbler of whiskey.

The man looked around the room, letting his eyes adjust to the dim interior. Hector nodded back and turned towards the bar. The television chattered away behind the long, buffed counter, showing the morning news in Spanish. Five costumed people faced off against two dozen T.A.L.O.N. agents on the screen; a muscular woman in patriotic colors lifted a car over her head as her shadowy lizard sidekick hid behind her; a glowing man blinked out of existence to appear behind the agents; another woman who looked like she belonged in a biker bar gestured at a handful of agents and they were flattened to the ground; and a skinny, pimply-faced youth dressed in an ill-fitting red jumpsuit with yellow boots and belt sprayed what appeared to be butter from his hands, causing agents to slip and fall.

Looking down, Jack returned to his book, puffing on a pipe.

"¡Hola mi amigo!" Raul greeted with a wide smile from behind the bar. "¿Cómo estás?"

"Bien bien. Gracias. Y tú?" Hector took a seat at the bar, swiveling the stool so he could see the whole place. "Una cerveza, Pacifico, por favor."

"Of course, my friend," Raul reached into the cooler under the edge of the tiled bar. He opened the bottle, jammed a lime into the top, and passed it to Hector. Grabbing a bottle off the counter Raul set a shot glass beside it and poured a tequila also.

Hector pushed the lime into the bottle and pressed the beer to his lips, drinking deeply.

"What brings you here so early? Carlos and Diego don't even have the grill warmed up, and Geraldo isn't even here."

"You let him in, so it can't be too early for a drink and a smoke, eh?" Hector said with a shift of his eyes, indicating the guy at the table with the fedora.

"Oh, Jack?" Raul glanced at the man in the small booth across the room and rubbed his round belly. "You know Jack, he keeps odd hours. I don't think he's been to bed yet. But what about you? You aren't usually here this early. Need some chile toreados? I think I can get some of those for you."

"No thanks. Late night, been on a job."

"Oh, ho ho! Ok, I see why you need the drink now."

"I need a check cashed, too," Hector pulled the check from his pocket and slid it across the bar. "Can you help me out with that?"

"Oh yes," Raul smiled. He picked up the check and unfolded it. Looking at it for a moment, his eyebrows drew together. "I have most of this here, but the rest will have to be later today. I don't keep that much in my pocket, and if I do, it's mostly in ones."

"No problem, I know you will get it to me when you can. If I don't get it today, I will get the rest when I come back around."

Raul pulled a roll of money from his pocket and counted out hundreds, fifties, and twenties into stacks of a thousand each. He stopped when he had six stacks and only a few bills left in his hand.

Hector looked at the guy in the booth and back at Raul.

"Ah, don't worry about him;" Raul said with a laugh, "He's had to do the same more than once. Is that enough for now?"

"Yeah, that's plenty. Thank you, my friend."

"Oh, don't worry. It's no problem. What else do you need?" Raul tucked the check and the rest of his money roll into his pocket, patting it to make sure it was secure.

"Information," Hector put the shot glass to his lips and sipped the tequila. His eyes turned to the TV where the newscaster reported on the latest development with a case The T.A.L.O.N. Agency was pursuing; telling how they have found how to switch off the cancer gene and were now seeking victims of the disease to test it on. It wasn't an immediate cure, but it allowed the body to recover without radiation or chemical treatment. A related story followed about a man in Chicago with a glowing hand that could channel energy who had been apprehended by the Agency before he could do any damage, and everyone was safe.

The TV began talking about the weather in Arizona and Raul turned back to Hector.

"What sort of information do you need?" Raul asked.

"About them," Hector gestured to the TV with his chin. "They been around lately? Asking any questions here in town?"

"Yeah, Alfredo said they were around earlier last week, interviewing people at a climate change rally downtown," Raul leaned his elbows on the bar. "They were looking for some woman though, said she was an ecological terrorist."

"They ask about me, or anything to do with anyone who worked with them at one point?"

"I think so, but I don't know," Raul rubbed his belly again. "Maybe you should go see Eddie Gonzales. He usually hears about these things before me. And knows more."

"Ok, will do. Maybe a quick smoke before I run off."

"You know where the humidor is. Grab something, and one to take with you. You got it covered already."

Hector cut the engine of his bike in front of Gonzales's Tattoo Shop, and kick the stand down. Swinging his leg over, he set his helmet on the seat and looked around the parking lot. Three cars and two motorcycles were there to keep his hog company. He sauntered to the door and pushed into the well-lit interior. The buzz of tattoo guns hummed from across a short wall to his left.

A muscular blonde girl in a white tank top with a half dozen facial piercings smiled at him from across a glass display case.

"Hey there, can help you?" she asked with a quirky smile, lifting her cheek stud.

"Yeah," Hector returned her smile, "I need to see Eddie Gonzales, please."

"He's working on someone. Do you have an appointment?"

"Tell him Hogshead is here to see him."

The girl slipped from behind the counter and went into the maze of tattoo cubicles, and stopped at the last one in the line. Hector could hear her talking, and she returned a minute later.

"Eddie will be with you in a little bit. He's just finishing up a cover piece."

With a nod, Hector wandered over to the vinyl couch and sat down. Crossing his hands over his stomach, he leaned his head back and dozed off without trying.

"Sleeping, old man?" Someone kicked his boot.

Opening his eyes, Hector saw Eddie standing in front of him, smiling. Nodding and sitting up, Hector held out his hand to his friend.

Eddie grabbed it and helped pull him up, and into a brief hug.

"Good to see you, my brother," Eddie slapped him on the back. "Whatchu need? New ink, or maybe an eyebrow ring?"

"I can use a touch up on a piece, but I need information."

"Is this front room work, or back room?"

"Back room. Definitely back room."

Eddie led him to the familiar private room in the back and gestured to the table for Hector to lie down.

Hector peeled off his shirt, and stretched out on the cool vinyl surface.

Eddie took a seat on the backless stool and rolled to the table.

"Ok, I think I see the problem. Is it the bullet hole in the shoulder piece?"

"Yeah, and the Taser marks. Can you clean that up too?"

"Man, I can clean anything up," Eddie rolled to the cabinet to get the colors he needed. "Bit off a mess there. Bet there's a story to go with that."

"There might be, but I need information more than I need to tell a story. I'm looking to clean up my record with The T.A.L.O.N. Agency. I need a virus and word of where I can go to link up with their computers."

"Hmph," Eddie grunted, rolling back to the table to setup the gun. "Yeah, I think I can get something. What exactly are you looking to do?"

"Remove me from their computers, or at least corrupt the data so they have a harder time with my history, habits, skills, etc."

"You know, they'll still be able to recreate the information from their agents, news articles, and all that stuff."

"I know, and they probably have copies somewhere, but I can only do what I can do. And if I happen to clear a few other files while I am clearing mine, that's okay, too."

"Why did you ever work for them anyway?" Eddie asked as he tested the gun. "Ok, I am starting, ready?"

"Yeah," Hector said, pausing so Eddie could hit him with the first touch that always made him tense for a second. The needle touched his skin and the muscles jumped. With an outward breath, Hector relaxed, the familiar buzz and sensation settling in, the smell of alcohol in the air; Eddie wiped at his skin with the wet paper towel.

"I worked for them because I thought they really meant to do some good. After all, when they started they were all about curing genetic diseases through gene therapy, and using nanotechnology to fix injuries that no doctor with a scalpel or laser could touch. We saw the results; at least we thought we did. Once I worked for them though, I saw the deeper plans. Well, I did after two years when I ran across the records of the little old lady in Virginia whose blood could make super soldiers. Psychotic, and they died when she died, but they were super soldiers. Enhanced strength, speed, healing, and heightened senses. Too bad they were too pugnacious and had a taste for the blood of others."

"So what about the space dust? From that meteor storm that took out Cincinnati, Dubuque, Rome, Omsk, Shanghai, and part of India? Didn't that do some shit to people, making them super heroes or some shit?"

"I don't know. They covered that up pretty well, and then used it as a smoke screen to take blame for other things."

"Smoke screen," Eddie laughed, "that's funny coming from you. So, did it make super heroes?"

"I don't know. I think so, but I can't be sure if they just didn't blame their failures on it. Telling everyone it had microbes and bacteria on it that interacted with us at a genetic level. All I know is that they scooped up every piece of rock they could, and swept the rest under the rug."

"Hm, well I wouldn't mind having some super powers. Maybe to fly, or turn invisible."

"That's all an impossibility. They have invisibility, but it's by light reflecting nanobytes. Flying still relies on jet suits. Though, I did hear of someone they engineered a skin flap into, so they could glide. But he had to be naked so the flaps would extend, unless they used an armored mankini. That didn't make for an efficient soldier."

"I guess not!" Eddie laughed again, lifting the needle from Hector's back. "So what happened to that guy?"

"No idea, but it was at least a dozen people," Hector paused and the needle bit into his skin again. "From then on they left that sort of thing to animal testing. And raising cognitive abilities in their 'natural corps' so they take commands better. No one notices a stray dog with loose skin. Well, not until it leaps off a building and glides off.

"What I do know is that they have a hand in the tech corridor, the pharmaceutical industry, and more. They have larger plans, and want to control everyone who has any abilities, genetic or technology. Even if they were the ones that infected the people with their condition without consent or knowledge. Then again, I have a suspicion that some folks didn't get their abilities from The T.A.L.O.N. Agency. But that's where mine came from."

Three days later, Hector sat on his bike studying the complex through a pair of tronicnoculars. Adjusting the link to his cardphone, he superimposed the downloaded floorplan over the transmitted image. The building looked like any other warehouse, except for the tinted windows. The roof had small windowed – also tinted - sheds on each corner and another in the middle of the front, sides, and back. Interior floors showed on the building through the tronicnoculars, shadowy images in green. This building stood far enough away from the other warehouses that going from an adjacent roof to it was impossible without a flight suit. Even a grapple gun wouldn't bridge the gap - not that Hector had one of those. It was new, too. Three other warehouses had been demolished to build this one. It was branded with the big box store label, WalkenMart, on the side of the building and all dozen of the eighteen wheelers in its receiving bay. People liked to joke they named it that because it was always a huge walk whenever you went into one of the stores. These stores combined the largest hardware store, with the largest sporting goods store, with the largest grocery store, and home goods store into one building. Even the other big box stores stood in awe and fear of them, lobbying to shut WalkenMart down because it harmed their 'smaller' businesses.

Hector knew this wasn't a warehouse full of household goods though; this was a laboratory. He had been in three of them before breaking away from the Agency to become hunted by them. It was in a place like this where he had been injected with nanites to create smoke clouds and embers by super heating the air and dust around him, and direct it. They'd enhanced his genetic code so he could filter and breathe the air he tainted, be resistant to the heat he could generate, and gave him gear that could do the same. Adjusting his link, he zoomed into the interior rooms with the superimposed silhouettes of employees taken from his security hack.

Listening to the police scanner on his cardphone through the earpiece, he learned that the local police would not respond to any call from this building. It had its own private security - security that Hector had once trained before he became Hogshead. Settling in, Hector waited for night to fall and the shift change.

"Easy, that's how it should be," Hector tucked the few tools he needed back into the tool bag. The guard behind the monitor smiled back and nodded.

"Yeah brother, if it could only be that way, my life and job would be so much easier."

"Pardon me, Officer Lee" Hector came behind the security desk beside the walk-through scanner. The guard moved to one side, allowing Hector access to the computer. "I just need to install the update, and I'll be done."

"Why didn't they send it down from headquarters in the middle of the night, like they usually do?"

"Because this update is meant to keep folks from hacking in, so they want it installed at the source and not brought in via hackable sources from the outside. It makes it just that much more secure."

The man nodded, as if it made sense, not wanting to admit his ignorance.

Hector brought up the configuration prompt of the Portals operating system, and popped in the travel hub he had brought, smiling at the small device that surpassed the old thumb and jump drives from years ago.

"I still don't know how they do that," the guard shifted, attempting to make conversation to stave off the boredom.

"Do what?" Hector clicked on the angled keyboard, his fingers tapped on the perfectly flat surface.

"Fit so much onto something the size of a postage stamp."

"Oh, yeah. It's cool isn't it?" Hector smiled up at the man, who watched the screen as he typed. "Since they finally got the graphene out things sure have changed. Phones the size of a credit card. Driver's Licenses that hold your full medical, criminal, school, and job history. Keyboards as thin as sheets of paper, and you can even roll them up and put them in a pocket. And these travel hubs that have the same storage as a full home computer from the mid-teens, but forty times the processing power. And thank goodness for LiFi, right?"

"I hear you!" the guard agreed. "I barely remember the days of WiFi; I was just a kid when they phased that out."

Hector glanced up at the man, guessing that he was the same age by the time he had been in the military for seven years. The graphene contact lenses in his eyes recorded it as video, and brought up a heads up information on the man showing his two years in the Army, and then a string of different jobs until he landed the job here twenty-six months ago. It also showed that he was chipped and each gun he had registered to that ID chip; the one on his hip was company-issued, and not linked to him. With a few keystrokes, Hector deactivated the magnetic finger lock on the man's sidearm. A lot had changed in fifteen years. "Yeah, a lot comes with change. Hell, T.A.L.O.N. is introducing a new pill this month with preprogrammed nanites that will do various tasks."

"Oh, I heard about that. My girlfriend wants one that will change her eye color with the app on her cardphone. I want to get my mother one that will find her arthritis and ease the pain when it flares."

"Sounds like you're a good son," Hector entered codes when prompted to install the software. In reality, it would make him invisible to any sensors in The T.A.L.O.N. network, including linked scopes. A few more moments and he had rerouted trigger-lock sensors to back flood if the weapon was pointed at him. "Ok, looks like I'm done here. You have a good night."

Hector held out a hand to the man, who gripped it in a handshake. Holding the hand firmly, Hector pulled the man forward, causing the man to stumble into him. With his left hand Hector grabbed the man's holster and pulled the trigger on the man's gun, and pushed him away in the same movement so they weren't making contact. The electronic safety guards on the weapon activated, sending a pulse of electric through the security guard. The man dropped to the floor, unconscious.

"Sorry, my brother," Hogshead whispered, pulling the unmoving form under the desk behind the security wall. "The headache will pass, and if they fire you, find something that doesn't darken your soul quite as much as this."

Peeling the jacket from the man, Hogshead removed his own and folded and tucked it beneath the man's head. He slid the newly acquired jacket on, and emptying the tool bag he turned it inside out, transforming it into a black cloth computer case. Returning the tools to inside pockets, Hogshead kept out his DMR and slung it over a shoulder. Checking the digital readouts on his eye contact lenses, he synced the weapon with the cardphone.

Setting an 'Out to Lunch, Will Return in 30 Minutes' sign on the desk, Hogshead set out for the service elevators. Nodding at the janitor he passed, and smiling at the few night lab techs, he made his way through a maze of corridors. Checking doors like any security personal would do, he passed through the facility without raising suspicion or alarm. No one questioned a man who belonged, even if his weapon wasn't the sort they were used to seeing. Once in the elevator, he checked his gear one last time before the doors opened onto the seventh sublevel basement.

The map on the readout of his contact showed the mainframe down the hall. Walking at a casual pace from one pool of light to the next, every third overhead light shining like streetlights from a childhood memory, he made his way to a door, machinery humming behind it. With a flick of his wrists a card popped from his left cuff, and a lock pick set from the right. Holding the card against the retina and fingerprint scanner, he manipulated the thin metal slivers into the physical lock. The door clicked open with an electronic ding, and he slipped inside, returning his tools into the wrist holsters.

With a sigh of relief, he walked to one of the three computer terminals. Things had changed a lot, but not at all since computers were first used decades ago. He slid into a chair, moving his finger over the light pad that had replaced a hand-held mouse years ago and the holomonitor glowed to life in front of him. The 3D image showed files layered deep. He flipped through the electronic folders, the images changing with each touch. Once he found what he was looking for, he pressed the icon to bring up the keyboard on the graphene desktop surface.

Setting the travel hub with the coding he had gotten from his contact, it linked and began deleting information related to him while uploading files on known modifieds, people who The T.A.L.O.N. Agency had encountered or altered. He had added some extra instructions, and it uploaded extra information about him and dozens of others, overwriting and sending out the misleading data to the network to be distributed. Exactly ninety seven seconds later the computer showed the transfers were complete, including the information that the data had been entered at twenty-three different locations around the world.

Retracing his steps, Hogshead reached the main level without encountering anyone. Leaving by his secondary route - so he wouldn't have to pass by the security checkpoint he had disabled thirty minutes previous - he entered the parking garage. A dozen men in riot gear waited for him, six kneeling, and six standing behind them, all with rifles aimed at his chest. One man stood to the side, hands clamped behind his back. His crisp military-style uniform showed him to be in command.

"Hogshead," the middle-aged man's voice as sharp as the ironed creases in his trousers, "you have been caught committing industrial espionage, trespassing on a private facility, theft of intellectual assets, and destruction of private property. You are to be detained and arrested."

"Bob Lowell," Hogshead sneered, "did they promote you? Was it the El Salvador operation, or the Paris one that got you this? And I didn't destroy anything."

"Oh, the destruction of private property hasn't happened yet, I'm just hoping you resist arrest. Then we can charge you for any damage done as we take you down. And we both know that neither your modifications, nor your gear, will withstand bullets, shock stock bursts, and the other things these boys will throw at you."

"You have no proof of anything, except I walked out this door."

"We may not have anything on camera, thanks to your clever trick of making the sensors not notice you, but we do have doors opening by themselves, computers activating with no one in the room, and a dozen or so eye witnesses that collaborate your whereabouts within the building." Lowell smiled, his eyes squinting. "So, it's your choice, but I encourage you: resist."

The two men stared at each other, the sound of creaking kevlar and shifting weapons coming from the twelve men covering Hogshead.

Hector's weapon bumped against his hip on its sling, as he dove to the left, away from where Lowell stood. Shots cracked and echoed in the concrete box of the garage as the men followed his path. No cars were close to the door, having been moved before he came out, but he headed for a thick concrete column. A bullet bounced off his plasteel shin insert, one embedded in his chest armor, and a third bit through the heel of his boot as he recovered his feet behind the concrete pillar. Dust and sand burst into tiny fires and a thick gray haze grew from thin air. Hogshead called upon his abilities to provide cover. Bullets whizzed past, skipping across the pavement in a shower of sparks; Hogshead blossomed them into an ember storm in the smoke cloud.

"Respirator masks!" Reynold's command was muffled as if he had already donned his own. "Use the spectral vision enhancement; don't rely on your own eyes or IR to find this bastard. Take him down! I want him alive!"

Grabbing his rifle from behind him, Hogshead clicked the safety off and chambered a round. Reaching into the black bag slung across his shoulder, he snatched out an attachment for his weapon and slid it into place along the track. The connection lit up in his heads-up display, showing the grenade launcher was live and the electric pulse was also. Looking up, he searched for pipes he could charge with the pulse option. But this was a modern garage, and though equipped with chargers for the cars, no conduit ran in visible places. Instead, he aimed for the lights and flicked the switch. Electricity arced from his weapon, LED lights overhead popping and exploding in a shower of sparks before they went dark.

Hogshead crouched and ran towards the line of cars thirty meters away, firing rounds towards the line of soldiers. A certain peace fell across him; there was no more worry, tension, or anxiety. Things were moving now; it was do or die time, and that is not the time to think things over and get stressed. He moved without thought, reacting as much as planning, reaching the next place and throwing down his next attack or throwing up his next defense without planning it. It was the dance of give and take that he knew the steps of, all too well.

One of the agents fired a magnetic grenade, and it rocked a car, attaching to it with a metallic thump. A sonic pulse accompanied the electro-magnetic pulse, throwing off his inner ear and his balance.

Hogshead stumbled sideways between two cars, hand reaching out to steady himself, and missing the hood of the car. He fell to the ground, shoulder crunching under his weight. The guns fell silent; the high pitched keening in his ears grew louder. A muffled voice broke through the wall of sound.

"Your nanites don't like that EMP, do they Hogshead?" Lowell shouted, his voice distorted. "And you can't handle SES bombs better than anyone else. Oh, SES is short for sonic equilibrium stasis, basically a dampening field that messes with your head and you can't tell up from down. You might even vomit."

Hogshead tried to find the voice, but the sound bounced off everything, like he was in an underwater cave of metal. He could see the SES grenade attached to the side of the car, but when he reached for it his hand went in the wrong direction. He could see the men closing in, moving forward in sets of three, taking new positions. Their headgear must have protection.

Hogshead fired wildly, causing the approaching men to take cover. With his free hand, he thumbed the music player on his phone and flicked the volume up to max. His earbuds flared to life, drowning out part of the disorienting noise from the SES.

Standing, one hand held out for balance, Hogshead stumbled away, firing blindly behind him. Sparks flew around him; garbled shouts came from behind him.

The disorienting sound cut off.

A blue glow enveloped the transmitter grenade on the side of the car, swallowing it and leaving a dent with a hole where the device had been anchored. The keening noise disappeared. Hogshead struggled to his feet, and a second, but identical, blue flicker above Lowell attracted Hogshead's eye.

The device that had disappeared a moment before dropped from the glowing hole, spike first, and embedded itself in the shoulder of the senior agent. The man screamed, clutching at his shoulder, falling over as the sonic waves overcame him and overpowered his ear protection. The agents in riot gear shouted and scrambled at their head gear; the signal must be transmitting through their comms.

A hand gripped his left bicep.

Hogshead flipped onto his back, turning his gun towards the new attacker.

A man in a brown leather coat and fedora with a goatee pushed the barrel to the side, Hogshead recognized him from the cigar lounge earlier.

"Come on," Jack pulled him to his feet, "let's get out of here before they turn that thing off and it gets messier."

Hogshead nodded, and scrambled after the man, who still held his arm to keep him steady. A blue portal opened in the air in front of them, just large enough for them to crawl through.

And they did.

"It's not the American Dream anymore," Jack sipped on a whiskey in a booth in Los Portales Oscuros.

Hector sat across from the man, drinking a Sol, smoking a thick cigar, and watching Raul count down the register. Empty plates sat on the table, scraps of tacos carne asada and arroz con pollo congealing on them.

"It hasn't been for a long time."

"How did you do that? The door in the air thing, I mean." Hector had fully recovered, his arm in a sling, and his damaged gear sitting next to him with his rifle.

"It happened back in 2012, when the LHC went live." Seeing the man's confusion, he went on. "The Large Hadron Collider, the machine meant to study the building blocks of everything. It opened an awareness in my mind, a sensitivity to, well for lack of a better word, wormholes. I can open them and travel through them. Lots happened then. That's when The T.A.L.O.N. Agency ramped up everything, from pharmaceuticals to graphene."

"You would have been a kid," Hector said.

"Well, I'm older than I look. Let's just say that traveling agrees with me and keeps me young. Anyhow, I have a strong sense of fairness and justice, so when I caught wind of what you were doing; I thought you might need backup."

"Raul talked?"

"No, not at all. But he knows me, and might have if I asked. He looks out for you. He's a good man."

Hector nodded and drew deeply on his cigar, leaning back and letting a thick cloud out, which he dissipated into the air with a thought, before it reached the other man.

"I found out through other means," Jack went on, "and did what needed done. So, what is next for you?"

"First, I need to get my bike. I parked it far enough away it should be safe."

"It is, Eddie's bringing it here right now."

"You know Eddie too?"

"We have quite a few friends in common, and they all look out for you. You've earned their loyalty, because apparently you're a good man, too, Hector."

"Well, in that case, I'll check the info I took and begin throwing a wrench into their future plans."

Hogshead walked away from his bike, towards the mall. The information on his cardphone said a kid named Robert would be inside. The Agency had programmed him through certain VR games to test new gear, and he would be preparing to use a certain weapon on unsuspecting people inside.

Hector was here to save lives, including the kid's, before he shot up the place and killed dozens.

"They won't stop on their own," he mumbled, "so someone has to stop them. And that someone is me."

People streamed out the doors, screaming.

It looks like things have already begun, he thought. Hogshead fought his way through the crowd, like a salmon swimming up a stream of humanity. Inside the air-conditioned interior, a series of explosions sounded from deeper inside the mall, and smoke billowed out. He reached out with his mind, giving himself cover in the cloud, running to do what needed done.

Travis I. Sivart

CASE 5392
CODENAME: LINE OF SIGHT

The sound of water tinkling and deflecting off the marbled squares in the manmade creek going down the center of the upscale outdoor mall was interrupted by the harsh trill of the alarm. The spring sun shone down between the buildings onto the blossoming shrubs and grass, the little train pulling children and adults from one end of the shopping plaza to the other slowing to a halt, parents grabbing their kids and fleeing for the exits to the parking lot. Men with guns stepped between the shoppers and escape, making the suburbanites backpedal and seek cover in stores, or nooks and crannies behind pillars or columns.

One man sat with his red tipped white cane in the metal chair outside The Cheesecake Factory, head tilted in a sunbeam and eyes hidden by dark glasses, listening to the commotion. Moments ago it had been the pleasant sounds of afternoon work lunches and mothers on an outing with over privileged children. The sound of people eating, guffawing between bites, and slurping on drinks that clinked with ice.

The noises of people eating reminded him of the time he had visited his grandparent's farm. He cringed at the sounds of people - like hogs, like locusts - devouring. The wet smacking noises of them masticating combined with the dry cracking sounds of the crisp bits being wolfed down. There was nothing he could do to stop it. He couldn't yell at them, couldn't beg them to stop, or scream at them to be silent. Not without him being the crazy one instead of them. But they didn't know they were crazy. He knew. He knew the insanity of others all too well.

The mall descended into a variety of insanities. With a sigh, he opened his mind to the vision that he had. The jarring scene of a tired thirty-something mother, in her beige capris and plain frosted lime V-neck t-shirt sprang into view in his head. She ran in a crouch, holding her bags to her chest, stopping behind a round stone planter, too afraid to peek out from behind it.

From his quick impression he knew she was a stay-at-home wife whose children had just begun school and she was enjoying some freedom. The rings spoke of money, and the manicured nails and stylized hair told the story of paying someone else to do her grooming. Poor people didn't do that, and they wore sweats and t-shirts with bands, movies, or stupid pictures and sayings.

People with money, wearing clothes with perfect seams and crisp folds, sporting fashions that anyone without money would scoff at; like the young woman fleeing, her glassy metal and plastic shoes linked together with what resembled the pedal assembly on a bicycle, causing her to lift and set her feet down in an exact spot dictated by the interlinked shoes. A slightly overweight, middle aged man stood still, trash bag wobbling in his grip, frozen with it halfway out of the can in the center of the mall walk. The wealthy didn't notice his grayed collar and sleeve cuffs, nor how he and others had waxy and sallow skin, instead of the healthy shine and polish of someone who could afford fresh produce and meat that hadn't been processed and blended.

He mentally leaped to the crouched woman's view, seeing through her eyes.

A man ran by her, scuffing his polished leather shoes, tripping over his own feet. His blue-striped dress shirt had a white collar, and his pastel pink tie flew over his shoulder. His hair didn't move - it was perfectly styled - and the glint of gold of his watch said he bought want he wanted without worrying. The man looked at the woman and then at the exit.

The woman watched him as he turned away from his only escape route, swearing.

They both swore.

The blind man could hear the words, battered down by the mall alarm, the two people hesitating in their fear.

"Mister," a female voice came along with a touch on the blind man's arm, "it's Amy, your waitress. You should come inside."

"Mark," the blind man corrected. He switched to the waitress's eyes, seeing himself and the whole outdoor courtyard. The waitress's eyes scanned the scene: urban terrorists and socialites alike. No one looked at him, their eyes slid past him, avoiding looking at him.

Most vision impairments could be corrected these days, so less people saw someone with his particular handicap.

This girl did though, watching his upturned face as he cocked his head to catch the sound of her voice better. He saw himself; dark hair cut short, plain white short-sleeve button-up shirt, and khaki pants.

"What?" She asked.

"My name is Mark, and I'll be fine. No one will bother a blind man. Thank you, Amy; you should go now, though. They will notice you."

"Ok," was all she said, and she turned and ran, crouching as she making her way between metal wire tables to the door into the restaurant.

Mark saw other employees and customers pressed to the sheet glass windows, watching the scene outside. It was nice that someone checked on him, but he wasn't surprised that it was an employee. He wasn't sure if it was the training, or just in the nature of people who worked with the public, but they were always the ones that tried to assist him. They weren't as pretty and tidy as the other people, and they smelled earthier, full of the scents of food, thick perfumes and cologne, and more. They weren't as thin as the people with money either, always a bit more padding. More natural; less sculpted.

He preferred them over the others. They looked at him, but people who felt entitled avoided doing so, as if they felt guilt for having something he didn't. But they ignored others who had everything they did, except money.

Through Amy's eyes, he watched himself; inside now, safer, as she looked around. There were two men with some sort of automatic rifles to the right, blocking the exit. The men spoke into radios. They wore black polo shorts and black work pants, very like a uniform. Their haircuts were military in style, and their skin was well tanned. That was all Mark saw through Amy's eyes before she turned away, heading towards the kitchen. He lost contact when she went behind the stone wall of the restaurant.

It was always like that since he figured out he could see through other people's eyes, after he lost his sight in the war in Chile. He had been blind for almost five years now, and surgery couldn't repair the damage, and his body rejected any nanite or electronic devices. Even the miracle workers at The T.A.L.O.N. Agency couldn't put him back together again, not completely. Something about his natural electromagnetic field being skewed in such a way it interfered.

Mark jumped into the vision of one of the men with black shirts and guns. The man stood still, and Mark had a good, steady view of the surroundings.

Dozens of people scurried about looking for hiding places. The man glanced down at his radio, and Mark saw the frequency they were using when the man brought it to his face to speak. A map of the mall came into view on a cardphone, showing two red dots at most of the exits, and a dozen more patrolling the open areas. These intruders had effectively locked down the whole mall with just over thirty men.

"May I have your attention, please," a deep masculine voice resonated over the mall's loud speakers, "we have hidden a dozen bombs throughout this mall. We will set them off if anyone attempts to leave or enter. We have notified the police of this, and expect them to meet our demands soon. When they do so, then you all may leave without any harm done..."

In the distance gunshots sounded and the PA system went quiet, followed by screams.

Mark jumped from one person's vision to another's, trying to find someone who could see what happened. Unable to find a suitable view, he switched back to one of the men guarding the nearest exit. The man spoke into his radio, his vision bobbing as he nodded his head. His gun came into view and he and his companion fired into the scattered crowd.

Panicked screams filled the air.

"Someone has just tested our resolve," the voice reverberated through the loudspeaker, "and they will no longer be putting anyone else in danger. Just stay where you are, don't try to run or hide. Sit down and keep calm, and no one will get hurt. Unless the authorities don't do as requested, of course. We have jammed all mobile devices and it would be best if everyone would just sit quietly until this is resolved."

Mark had the urge to leap up and do something. He had always been strong and independent. Thirteen years in military service and a half dozen awards showed that. He wasn't one to sit and wait. He had lived a good life, and had friends and family around him. He went out and got what he wanted.

Now he was forgotten. Friends had faded away and family had grown older, needing to put their own needs before his. People wouldn't even make eye contact with him when he couldn't see. These people wouldn't help him cross a street, he had no obligation to do anything for them. His mother had always said that the strong should protect the weak, and you should always help those who needed it.

Now, the ones who could do anything wouldn't. They cowered and hid.

Mark hid in plain sight. He could do what these people couldn't. He could behave without fear, because no one feared a blind man. All he had to do was figure out what these men wanted.

In the distant past he had dealt with men that relied on violence and intimidation. It was rare that they wanted what they said; it was almost always a front for their true motives. If he could figure out what they wanted, how would he get that information into the hands of people that could use it?

Popping a bite of seasoned fries into his mouth, the blind man stood. Flicking the cane forward, he stepped sideways from between his chair and the table. Turning to his right, he headed for the gate he had heard opening and clanging closed earlier.

Mark jumped from person to person, using their sight to see where he could not. He jumped further away from himself, trying to see around distant corners distant to verify what he had seen on the cardphone of the men in black polo shorts. Normally, he did this while still, and doing it while walking was disorienting. It was like a man walking across the top of a moving train in those old movies, jumping to the next car, and then leaping to another train headed in the opposite direction. Mark smiled, remembering the old cartoons his Pap had watched, where a flea would leap from one dog to another. He felt like that and he walked with jerky motions, stumbling as he hadn't done since he'd first lost his sight.

People stared at him; he could see their faces through others' eyes. They were amazed and terrified. They twitched, wanting to pull him down, but too afraid to do so. He made his way down the sheltered walkway. The sound was all wrong too, like watching a movie out of sync with the audio. The people watching him saw his cane clicking on the concrete, but he heard it a second before they saw it connect.

He collected details from the attacker's eyes, and the people watching them. They were all dark of skin and hair, though clean shaven. They had to be para-military from their stance, weapons, and matching outfits. Mark doubted they were here for money. They hadn't approached a single store, or taken a single item from anyone. With that thought, the PA blared to life again.

"Your attention, please," the same deep voice said, "a young lady will be coming around to collect wallets, phones, and jewelry. I suggest you fill her shopping bag quickly and generously. If she does not return to us with satisfactory amounts of items, we shall shoot her as punishment. Then each guard shall shoot one person in the leg, at random. Thank you for your cooperation."

People hesitated, shuffling jewelry to their pockets as he watched from a teen clerk's eyes within an upscale sports store window. These people would get themselves, and others, killed over a few trinkets that could be replaced.

Mark stopped, feeling a stone pillar with his hand then leaning against it, digging out his wallet and phone. He pulled off his military signet ring, and held the items in front of him, waiting for someone to come by and collect it.

While waiting, he thought about the man on the loudspeaker. His voice was clean, almost without an accent. Whoever it was, he'd schooled himself to have a neutral tone and not be recognizable. It held no local inflection, and that meant this person was probably foreign and educated here in the States.

Time stretched on. Someone collected items, a meek female voice asking and apologizing in the same breath. The sound of metal and plastic in a soft-sided reusable shopping bag echoed off the open sided stony corridor. Mark reached out with his mind and jumped to someone's vision as the woman spoke to him, asking for his valuables. The girl was young, somewhere this or that side of drinking age. He considered her, and decided the men chose her specifically because of her skin tone and attitude. It would give the people sympathy towards them if someone like themselves did this. He watched himself drop his possessions into the waiting sack. The woman thanked him, all as he spied on his own interactions.

The girl left to collect items from the next person, laid on the ground under a stone bench, huddled close to his child.

Mark turned and walked away, his cane clicking, swaying in front of him, a metronome for his steady pace. He kept his mental perception flicking from person to person, watching the scene around him. Reaching the stairs, stone platforms open to the ground behind them; he climbed them with one hand on the rail and the other holding the cane vertically to measure the steps' height. Reaching the top, he searched for eyes to see through. There were less people up here, and fewer guards. Mark latched on to the vision of one of the men with a rifle, and saw himself in the center of the image. Turning, the blind man clicked his way in the opposite direction.

Once the man was lost behind a corner, Mark's vision went black. He sought out another set of eyes, but the upper level was deserted enough that he was alone in the area.

He sat on a bench, brought out a small notepad and a pen from the breast pocket of his shirt, and began to write. He kept it slow and methodical, so it was legible as possible, and used his finger as a guide along the paper's edge to keep the lines relatively straight. Mark recalled the shapes of letters; it wasn't that long ago that he used them on a regular basis in reports and whatnot. He had considered using braille, but it would take too long for law enforcement to translate it without the proper app on their cardphones. As he wrote, the PA burst to life again.

"May I have your attention, please." It was a statement, not a question. "It seems some folks have held back and didn't contribute to the collection as they should have. Because of your selfishness, the lovely young lady who took up the collection will be executed. Bring her forward." The girl could be heard, weeping and begging, in the background of the announcement. "Hold her still, I don't want to get one of you by mistake."

The retort of a gun echoed off the walls from the PA and elsewhere, the sobbing and screaming stopping at once. In the surreal silence breathing could be heard over the speakers. "I hope this shows our sincerity and conviction. Now, each guard will single out one person and shoot them in a non-lethal manner. Dependent on you, if someone decides to run, or resist, or help another, then the bullet may go astray and do more than wound. There is also the chance that the authorities do not acquiesce with our demands in an expedient manner, thus causing someone to bleed out and die from their injury before help arrives. I recommend complete subservience; your lives depend on it. Cooperation is key, and resistance may lead to your death."

Mark scanned for available eyes to use while the voice droned on in its overly non-accented manner. No one was close. He recalled a metal railing between buildings that overlooked a parking lot. The police would have eyes on those sort of exits and would probably see what he did there. Folding the paper in a very specific way, Mark then stood up and tapped his way to the access point he recalled. The intensified breeze from between the buildings on his face, told him that he was close. The retort of weapons echoed off the walls again as the terrorists followed through with their leader's promise and shot innocent bystanders.

Seeking people around him one more time, Mark reached out for eyes to look through. He found a set ahead of him, but quite a distance away. Jumping into the person's vision, Mark saw himself very close up through the tronicnoculars the man was using. The view was disorienting and he saw himself catch at the railing with one hand as he nearly fell. He watched himself pull out the folded paper as he felt his hands doing it, unfolding it to a triangle shape and releasing the paper airplane. The note flew straight and true, catching an updraft, and passing the first rows of vehicles before drifting below the electronic binocular's field of vision and settling to the ground.

The crackle of a radio sounded from behind, surprising him. The man whose eyes he had been using had shifted the electronic binoculars to follow the path of the paper airplane, so Mark could no longer see himself. Shifting his awareness to the person behind him, he saw a hand reaching for his own back and grab his body by the shoulder. The blind man was yanked backwards, his vision steady as the world shook violently around his body. The disorienting effect made his gorge rise, and he barely kept his recent meal down. He hit the ground hard and was dragged backwards, kicking his feet and trying to gain purchase.

The ground fell away from underneath him and he tumbled backwards and down, rolling head over heels down sharp concrete stairs. He attempted to protect his head with his arms, and his cane flew from his hand. He heard a sickening crunch and pain blossomed in his right wrist and forearm as he hit the edge of a stair with them before coming to land on the arm on flat ground. Mark heard the sound of multiple booted feet around him, but couldn't pull his focus together enough to borrow a set of eyes to see what was going on.

"I have sent the live security feed to the TVs around the mall," came the masculine voice over the loudspeakers, "so you may watch what happens when someone disobeys. There will be no mercy whether you are a woman, or even blind. Gentlemen, please discipline the dissenter."

Booted feet met Mark's ribs, face, legs, and groin, men gathering around kicking him. The butt of a gun hit his temple and the world spun in the darkness. Pain radiated from his broken arm, further disorienting him. It seemed endless once it stopped. Mark had no idea how long it continued. He had endured worse in the past, but that was a distant memory and this was now. The pain, humiliation, and frustration was now. He heard the men breathing heavy from their exertion and a woman sobbing somewhere nearby. He reached out, trying to gain use of a set of nearby eyes. A white light of intense fire shot through his head, splitting his efforts like a hot knife through frozen butter. He failed. Instead, he lay there on the ground, trying to recover and breathe.

The men walked away, their boots echoing, crisp steps receding. They didn't shuffle, but stepped with confidence. These were not casual people; they were trained. The thoughts came to Mark through the haze of pain, and he realized he had to do more. Sitting up, the world spun again and his stomach twisted. He lurched sideways and got sick; trying to make sure it flew away from him and not onto him. He lay still, and then reached for his mouth with care, using his left hand. His lip was swollen and his face bloody. Wiping with the back of his hand, the warm liquid mixed with his vomit.

Slapping the concrete, he listened. The sound echoed around him, but less so in one direction. He pulled himself towards that duller sound, clutching his shattered right arm to his chest. Feeling ahead of himself, he reached with his left, using his battered legs to push himself along. His hand touched the rough, rounded texture of a column. Mark pushed himself against it, pressing his back to it. He steadied himself, leaning against the cool stone.

After a moment to catch his breath, he untucked his overshirt and pulled the bottom over his arm and shoulder, creating a makeshift sling. Folding his left arm, he shoved that hand into its own sleeve, and with a bit of wiggling was able to wriggle the arm out of the shirt, and push the shirt onto the left shoulder, completing the sling.

Reaching behind himself, he fumbled with his back pocket, stretching to reach the right side one, and pulled out his hanky with his fingertips. Leaning back exhausted from the effort, he caught his breath, his head spinning again. They had really done a number on him. He hadn't planned on that. They really showed the people they meant business. Waiting for the dizziness to pass, he thought through his plan again. The last move was idiocy, he decided. The police would have already known how many and the placement of the men through satellite imagery. But maybe he could turn this to his advantage anyway, and use his actions – and the enemies reaction – to inspire others to fight back.

"Water," Mark croaked, "can someone bring me some water?"

No movement sounded, and even the sobbing woman went quiet. He sighed. He should have known better. These people were used to everyone doing for them, protecting them, and didn't ever expect to have to do for themselves. The scrape of rubber on the pebbled ground came from his right. He turned his head away from the source, hoping to catch the sound better.

"No, Peter, wait!" said a young girl's voice.

The sound of someone moving towards him came closer. A hand touched his shoulder, gentle and cautious.

"Here," the high-pitched voice warbled. Mark wasn't sure if it was from fear or puberty, but he reached towards it and hit a water bottle with his knuckles. Fumbling, he shifted his hand to find the waiting container. He set it on his thigh, and moved his hand upward, feeling at the top to figure out how it opened.

"Oh, sorry man. Let me help."

The kid held the bottle with one hand, and flipped the tip back with the other. Then he took Mark's hand and placed it on the open top so he could feel what was what.

Mark smiled, his face cracking. Raising the bottle to his face he poured some into his mouth, then across his face, swallowing. A second, lighter, set of sneakers approached.

"Peter, we can't help him," a high-pitched voice quavered.

"Yes, we can," Peter answered, "and we will. You gotta help others, because if you don't, then why should anyone… oh, never mind Mindy. You wouldn't understand."

"That's not fair," Mindy said, "I'm old enough to understand. I just don't think it's smart."

"Hey, kids," Mark poured some water on his hanky and wiped his face, "thank you. Thank you both. You're both very brave, and smart for helping me."

"Don't worry about it man," said the teen boy.

"Why was it smart?" Mindy asked. "They might come out and stomp us now."

"Because I am going to help you get out of here, without getting hurt. That's why. I know how. But, I need you two to be my eyes. Can you do that?" The two kids shuffled and Mark guessed they were looking at each other to gauge the other's reaction. Mark wrapped the hanky around his broken forearm and pulled it tight, grimacing. Forming a loose knot, he pulled it tight with his teeth and pressed back against the column with his feet, trying to stand. "Help me up, and get me to a wall near a store, make it a boutique, one for women, with large windows. Can you do that?"

"Yeah," Peter said, "I guess so."

"Good," Mark reached for Peter. He touched the boys shoulder. The kid was about a foot shorter than him, but it would work. And the physical contact allowed him to make a visual connection. Images of himself swam in his mind, the boy staring at his broken and bloody face. "Peter, let me lean on you a bit. More to guide me, but also to make sure my legs are steady. I shouldn't be too heavy; I think I can walk ok."

Mark positioned himself to lean on the kid a bit, and pivoted the boy towards a purse store.

"Is there a women's store that way?" Mark gestured with his chin towards the store he could see through Peter's eyes.

"Yeah, it's a…"

"Doesn't matter. Mindy, lead the way. You're doing great."

The girl led the way, with the two men in tow. Mindy grabbed Mark's cane in passing, and handed it back to him. He clutched it vertically against his chest, using his right hand to hold it as best he could, and kept his left on Peter's shoulder. Once they reached the glass storefront, Mark leaned against the windows, releasing Peter, and switched the cane to his left hand.

"Now, you two are going into the store, and I will create a distraction. You have to get to the back door. These men will have locked all the doors down with maglocks, standard mall security. Take this device, I am setting up an app that will give short electromagnetic burst. Put it on the back door lock, and activate it. It will clip the magnetic signal and let you shove it open. Once it is open, run. Run to the cops, and tell them that these men are on a private channel on their radios. They're using a ham radio signal, 1.835 MHz frequency. Can you remember that? It's a South American frequency used in, well, it doesn't matter. Tell the police to send a burst on that frequency and it should stun these guys through their Bluetooth receivers for a couple seconds and let them get the advantage. Can you do that?"

Mark saw the girl nod through Peter's eyes as the teen's own head went up and down too.

"I'll take that as a yes. Ok, sneak towards the store, once I start yelling, count to twelve, then go inside and make your way towards the back of the store and the back room. Try to stay behind the displays and out of sight."

"How can you know what radio frequency they're using?" asked Peter.

"I overheard them. Doesn't matter. Go. Get to safety, and if you do this, you'll both be heroes. Now, go!"

Mark shoved Peter away, towards the door. He watched through the kid's eyes as the two made their way.

Stumbling forward, trying to look injured and helpless – which wasn't very difficult considering his condition - Mark spoke in a loud voice, "Hey, people. These men are going to kill everyone, I know that, and you know that. The only chance we have is to fight back, that's the only way any one of you have the chance of surviving this. These men don't care about us, except as bait for their trap."

Mark saw his back when Peter glanced over his own shoulder to look behind him as the teen and the girl entered the store.

"You must stand up to them, or at least run and try to escape. Two kids had more guts than all of you combined, and helped me stand up, so I can stand against these men again. A blind man, who was beaten and thrown down stairs. I have a broken arm, and I am willing to stand up again."

"But you don't have kids!" A man yelled.

"You don't know that," Mark shouted back, "you don't know who is waiting for me at home. And I am asking you to give your kids the best chance at surviving this now, by doing something. Don't wait for them to come kill you! They've already shot dozens of people, why would you be any different?"

Peter looked one last time before going into the stock room. Through the teen's eyes, Mark saw his own back, and the armed men coming up behind him. He hoped the kid could pull this off.

Dropping to his knees, he swung his cane and connected with someone's legs. The man fell over and Mark dove towards the sound. Touching the man, he pushed into the man's sight and saw himself over the man. He punched into the man's face and the vision went dark. Mark snatched the fallen man's weapon and pulled it to him, feeling along the barrel for the safety. Releasing it, he opened fire in an arced spray around him. Other men shouted, leaping for cover. Pushing his senses into another soldier's eyes, Mark saw cover and scrambled for it, getting himself behind a solid stone column just before the remaining men began firing their weapons.

Mark reoriented his sight to a bystander crouched behind him, getting a teary view of the other men seeking a better position to shoot from. He fired at them, taking down two more, and pressed himself against the stone. The others returned fire. He only had to hold out for a few minutes, and the men shouldn't hit him. But there was always an unlucky shot, and that could end his plan before he could really get it moving.

Through the sobbing woman's eyes Mark saw a man in a business suit run for one of the fallen men's weapons and get cut down. Other people tried the same.

They were cowards and stupid, but at least they were trying and that would be enough of a distraction for the kids to get to the cops and the cops to do what they needed to do.

Soon the armed men were fighting a half dozen bystanders and were pinned down. More were coming, though, and the suburbanites were easy targets for the trained soldiers. The terrorists screamed and clutched their heads, falling to the ground, pulling the earpieces out of their ears. Men in uniforms rappelled down from above, and other in riot gear ran in through the gaps between buildings, rifles firing rounds into the attackers.

Ten minutes later Mark sat on the edge of one of the fountains, an EMT checking his arm. Twenty minutes later, he rested on the bumper of an ambulance, being interviewed by a police detective who wanted to know how Mark gave that information to the kids. How Mark knew the number of men and positions, and where they were from.

Mark explained how people ignore the blind, and how he overheard things even though he couldn't see a thing. He explained how he recognized Portuguese accents, and the men's speaking voices were controlled and bored, but not angry. That spoke of formal training. The men had key rings, which people in this country no longer used, but South Americans did. The ringtones were generic, like on burner phones. Americans all personalized theirs. He smelled the men's coffee, a South American blend, and the lingering scent of food, spices, and seasonings in the man's sweat, not to mention the colognes, which were an airport standard, from bathrooms. All these things carried on breezes and sighted people didn't recognize them. But a blind man did.

He watched the tablet the detective used, reading it through the man's eyes. Mark mentioned very specific people he had encountered while in the military and watched the cop pull up those people's records. He mentally filed the addresses, locations, and other information away in his mind. The detective finished his questions and moved on to the next person.

Mark stood, holding his cane. An EMT took his arm, attempting to help him enter the ambulance. Pulling his arm away, he smiled in the direction of the woman and shook his head. A horn blared.

"My ride is here," Mark said to the woman. "I will get treatment on my own; I signed the paper refusing treatment from you. It's ok. Just get me to that cab that just honked."

"How did you know that was a cab?" The EMT asked, looking around.

"Because I am expecting a friend to pick me up."

The woman nodded and guided Mark through the crowd, towards the waiting taxi. Mark slipped into her sight, and walked towards his ride. The door of the cab opened. A woman waited inside. The EMT released his arm and he settled himself in the car. The door closed and the cab pulled away.

"I'm glad to see you weren't hurt," Mark said to the woman.

"I'm sorry you were," the young dark-skinned woman answered, pulling his ring, wallet, and cardphone from a bag. "They shouldn't have been so rough."

"They were only doing their job. They did what was necessary. And I got what I needed." Mark leaned back, cradling his arm. Then he spoke to the tanned man in the black polo who was driving, "Take us home, Andre. We have a lot of work to do before this is all done. The police won't take down this man, so we will. And I will lead us into a new era."

CASE 2234
CODENAME: THE HAUNT

Jamie Erich was a man on a mission, and he would show them all. The non-descript man sauntered down the sidewalk, chewing on a toothpick, his hands tucked into the pockets of his grey Members Only jacket. The rain pattered down around, but barely touched him. Other people ducked their heads and walked with purpose, wanting to be out of the wet weather, little puffs of breath clouding the cold air in front of them. Cars hummed past, the sound blending with the deeper thrum of the elevated trains.

Bristol was never warm when he was a kid, but since the sea levels had risen due to the warming trend – that's what they called it now, and told everyone it was a natural cycle, but they should still cut energy use and fossil fuel, and all that crap - it kept humidity even more; thus, the cold was worse. Some streets had flooded and raised walkways erected so storefronts were now waterfront and basements had been flooded. That was until they had the city-wide pumping commission come in and reseal the bottom meter of every building and pump out all the flooded basements five years ago.

A pushchair slid sideways, away from Jamie's path. The mother looking around, startled, her head whipping back and forth for the cause. Jamie sniggered, made eye contact with the woman, and mouthed the word 'ghost', pointing at the well-preserved graffiti of Banksy, The Well Hung Lover, in the alley she was passing. The mother glanced behind her and turned back to him with wide eyes. Snatching up her child from the buggy, catching its foot in a strap and shaking it to free it, she pressed the kid to her breast and dragged the buggy behind, scurrying from the area.

Chelsie had dumped him, but he would show her too. She said she wanted someone to rescue her. Save her from all the horrible things of her childhood, the string of bad relationships she'd had, and from the boredom of a mundane existence. She said she wanted a knight on a white horse to ride in, a hero to swoop down and carry her away.

He'd done everything he could, but it hadn't been enough. He had to work, and he didn't get paid much. But she wanted him to spend all his time with her, and buy her dinner out most nights and buy her pretty things. She wanted him to want her, but not be jealous when she flirted with other men, telling him he was being silly and she was going home with him.

She'd wanted all these things and more, but she didn't want to do anything for it. Not clean up when he was at work. Not give him backrubs, or buy him nice things, or even do his laundry. She didn't even work, saying she was an artist and wanted – needed - to paint. Well, he had set her up with a studio in his flat, took up the whole dining area, it did. But she never painted anything. The stuff just sat there. She'd said she was too stressed out to be creative. What the hell did she have to be stressed about? The Old Couple show having marital problems? The thirty-whatever season of Doctor Who being delayed because the latest Doctor was arrested for indecent exposure? She didn't get that new handbag she wanted?

It didn't matter now, she had dumped him. Moved in with her girlfriend Miranda, an old lover, and become the third in the poly triad with some bloke named Johnny. Was he the hero she wanted? He would show them. She never believed in what he could do, but now he would show them all.

He had no family; his foster parents didn't want anything to do with him. Said he was too cold, too weird. They'd never understood him either. But he didn't need them. He lost all his friends when Chelsie came along; they'd all said he'd changed. Now he didn't have her, and she took away all his friends, too. He might be broken, but he would come out better for it. Stronger.

Stopping in front of the brownstone, Jamie reached out with his mind, searching. Imagining someone who was afraid, worried, scared, he sought out that set of feelings. Like a tug on a mental fishing line, there was a bite. He reeled in his awareness, not too fast; he didn't want to lose the connection.

"Got them!" he muttered, passersby staring at him as he passed.

A man leaned over to his lady and whispered, "Did you see that? That guy wasn't even getting wet from the rain!"

"Don't be silly, he must have just got out of a car, or come from inside." She said back to him, patting his arm.

"No, I saw him from way up the street, just standing there, staring at that building…"

The two passed out of range of earshot, and out of the range of his abilities to perceive their thoughts. He should have tripped the guy, and blamed it on entity activity. It would have helped support what was about to happen.

A woman – terrified – screamed inside the building; the sound was followed by children crying.

Jamie smiled and turned away, walking into the grey mist of the day.

The next day he returned, eating a sandwich, and stopped in front of the same building. Finding her mind, he hooked on again. Pulling harder, he sent waves of energy into her and back out of her. Something heavy crashed inside the building and the scream was heard again.

Jamie moved on. Tomorrow he would do something about it.

Three days later found him across the street, grey Members Only jacket pulled around him in the morning dew. A newspaper tucked under his arm had published an article about her haunted flat. She thought it was her dead father - a violent man. The sun would be out today, but that didn't matter. He found her without searching this time. Her mind was familiar. He stroked it. She was sleeping. He sent the energies in again, making it touch her this time. He didn't doubt that she woke most of the building with her screams. He would return later.

"Jamie Erich." he said, holding out his hand, "I believe you and think I can help."

"Amanda Tilton," the woman said, tucking a stray strand of dirty-blonde hair tinged with white behind her ear. "How did you hear about this? Was it the paper? They didn't give my address."

"Yeah, I saw it in the daily, but I could feel the energy when I walked past. I thought to myself, this must be the place. And I want to help."

"How. . ." Amanda looked over her shoulder at the two small children - two girls - behind her, "what can you do?"

"I am attuned to this sort of... disturbance. Can I come in?"

She moved to one side, gesturing for him to enter.

He stepped around her and over the toys littering the floor, keeping his hands held in front of him, like he was looking to warm them over a fire. The room smelled like sweat and cheap food that came from a box.

"Yeah, there's something here. It feels very angry, and powerful. I am getting something," he put a hand to his forehead. People always needed dramatics to believe he felt anything. "It's a masculine energy, and he feels like you. Maybe... your father?"

"Yes," she stumbled over the word, "my father died a few years back. He was always upset, and took it out on me and my sister when we were young."

"Well, we don't want your daughters to go through the same thing you did, do we now?" Jamie spoke with false sincerity. "I can remove him. I can place wards that will stop him from ever coming back, too, and even encourage him to move on to the next plane. Would you like me to do that?"

"Yes, please! Anything you can do, just help me!"

"Alright, I will need some compensation though," he turned to look at her.

Suspicion flared in her narrowed eyes.

With a mental nudge, magazines scattered from the coffee table and across the room.

"Ok, anything! I only have a few hundred, but I can give it to you."

"Good, and there is the confidentiality agreement. We will both agree not to tell anyone names or details about what happened here. I wouldn't want the press to bother either of us. I am sure you just want to get on with your life, and I just want to help."

Jamie walked down the street fingering the cash in his pocket, when heard a voice say, "Aren't you that guy I saw on this street a few days ago?"

Turning, Jamie saw the man who had been whispering to his girlfriend under an umbrella the first day he had found the house.

"I don't know, mate," Jamie smiled, "I don't tend to keep track of weirdos on the street."

"Well, I do, and it was you. What the hell are you doing back here?"

"A man's allowed to walk down a street, right? Nothing wrong with that, is there?"

"Depends on what he's doing on that street," the man stepped forward and loomed over Jamie. "What have you been up to?"

Holding up his hands, showing they were empty, Jamie reached behind the man with his mind, and tugged on the guy's shirttail. The man spun around, hands clenching into fists. Jamie tickled the man's belly with another gentle probe of telekinesis. The man leaped backwards, stumbling into Jamie and falling.

"Oh, you alright there mate?" Jamie reached down to help the man up.

"What the hell was that?" the guy's voice shook.

"I didn't see anything. You been drinking?"

"No, I ain't been drinking," the man yelled, slapped Jamie's hand away, and pushed himself to his feet.

Jamie caressed the man's ear with another tendril of thought.

The man leapt into the air, spinning around and slapping at the side of his head.

"Never mind," the guy panted, panicked, "I'm outta here."

With a smile, Jamie watched as the man run down the street, not once looking back. Today was a good day, and the beginning of a new world.

The husband and wife, Michael and Shirley Kinkaid, sat at their dining room table. She was crying into her hands and he was as white as a proverbial ghost.

Jamie stood across from the pair, hands in the pockets of his new peacoat, which was much warmer than his old jacket. Khakis had replaced his old jeans, and his haircut made folks more at ease than the shaggy look he'd sported not long ago.

"It's your children, isn't it?" Jamie asked. "I can feel them, they feel lost. Like they don't know where to go. I can help them. You saw my references."

The wife sobbed harder, and the husband nodded.

"I can free them from their pain. This is what I do, I help people. Do you want me to help them?"

"Yes," the husband whispered, his voice rasping. "We will pay the three thousand you ask, and sign the privacy agreement."

"Alright then," Jamie retrieved a folded paper from his coat with a pen and slid it across the table. After the couple signed, Jamie pulled the paper back and tucked it away. "Time to get to work, this won't take long."

Turning away from the couple, Jamie began undoing what he had set into motion a week before, releasing the psychokinetic energies he had placed throughout the residence.

Lucky thirteen; this one would be the big score. Jamie tucked the silk shirt into his trousers. Checking the mirror, he decided against a tie, but added a suit jacket and the long overcoat. He went easy on the jewelry though, if you looked too rich people didn't trust you. Just a simple gold cross and chain, and a white gold wedding band - people also trusted a widower who had lost his wife. They believed what they wanted to believe, and they ate it up when he told them about his own haunting.

One person said they had looked him up and he had never been married.

That was easy enough to dodge, though. He'd explained they'd had a small, country ceremony, and poor Lizzie died the next day when they were robbed in the hotel. Jamie even looked up a news story about something just like that and used the location to give it more realism. No names were mentioned anyway. No one knew the difference.

Petting his cat, Zazzles - he was careful not to get fur on his outfit – he checked his teeth in the mirror. They looked good, thanks to the dentist that he had got rid of a ghost for.

Looking around his new flat, which he had got at a steal from a banker he had exorcized a demon for, he smiled. Yes, he was on top of the world. Once he did this job, he would look at even bigger marks to fleece. Maybe Buckingham Palace needed a bit of his sort of help?

Locking the door as he left, the scanner glowing to the right of the door, he turned and headed to the waiting black cab. The cab pulled away heading for Deanery Road and College Street - just a couple blocks away from the first haunting Jamie had solved on Frog Street – where he would then go to Bristol Cathedral. He leaned back, reminiscing, the scenery shooting past the window of the vehicle.

This haunting was his pièce de résistance; demons inside a well-known church. He had started small, on a weekday. Sitting inside the Cathedral during an afternoon communion, watching the people move along the Stations of the Cross in silent meditation of Christ, he'd set the first haunts out to play. Little noises, like singing, or a candle blown out right after someone lit it. Christianity, and religion in general, had declined over the past couple decades, but enough people still showed up to make a good show. TV had ruined a lot, consistently showing no proof of hauntings or ghosts, but with Jamie's abilities, he had been able to bring a revival of sorts to occultism. He laughed at the play on words.

He had built on it after that, tying energies to each person he saw that appeared to be a regular parishioner, playing on their individual tenets. He tied the biggest haunts to the Canons, especially the Canon Precentor, Canon Chad Bovary, Canon Pastor, Canon Derek Nickels, and Diocesan Canon, Canon Stanley Roberts.

Within a week there were stories of demons screaming and throwing candles, Bibles, and crosses throughout the Abbey. Attendance of the regular congregation dropped, but tripled from curious busybodies. Pews would tremble then be thrown over by some invisible force, voices echoing from the arched ceilings overhead, and effigies of saints trembled when people drew close.

It was a beautiful thing!

Who could measure up to him now, Jamie wondered. What would Chelsie think of him? Could Johnny and Miranda compare to him? He didn't think so.

He laughed, the cabbie glancing in the rear view mirror, as he thought of all the money and power he had claimed. Poor Chelsie, she was missing out on so much. Soon the whole country would bow to him, begging him to come save it, one haunting at a time.

There had been press coverage and crowds of people. It wouldn't be easy to remain anonymous after this, but he had a plan for that, too. As simple as coming in the back door and the clergy keeping the public out for the time he was inside. He would be the mystery hero, the one man everyone wanted but no one knew. He would be strolling past the mass of inquisitive and worried spectators, and they would never know he caused the very thing they waited for him to fix, without even knowing he was there.

The black cab let him out two blocks from the Cathedral, scanning his card to take the fare. Jamie meandered down the sidewalk. The crowds were already there; throngs of people pushing against the police lines, men in dark blue holding them back from the holy house. Jamie smiled as he turned down a path of gravel and paving stones, heading for the back entry.

An intern let him in, a petite little redhead with a pixie nose and innocent smile that spoke of the urge to be tempted. He smiled at her and chucked her under the chin with two fingers and winked as he passed, perhaps closer than socially acceptable.

But she didn't mind. She was in awe of him, they all were. Men in long religious garb surrounded him, wringing their hands, like nervous birds, asking him if he would be able to dispel the disturbances. He guaranteed them he would, and assured them that the press and church never had to be the wiser of his presence.

Jamie went to the center of the main chapel and ringed himself in candles, lighting each as the priests prayed around him.

He asked them to intone the saints to protect and guide his hand.

They did as he asked; sibilant whispers echoing off the walls and high ceilings.

Jamie gestured, telling spirits to be gone and not interrupt his holy duties. He began disconnecting the ties of energies from each man and the locations where he had planted psychic disturbances.

He wrinkled his forehead; not everyone was here. He couldn't untie what he had set if the people weren't here.

With a shrug, he set dampeners on the other places where he had set the telekinetic triggers, hoping it would disburse the energies when the people came in later.

Wandering from chamber to chamber, he continued to release what he had planted. The main doors opened and five people entered, three men and two women, all in dark suits. He heard the words 'T.A.L.O.N. Agency' as they showed identification to the Canon who greeted them.

The man nodded and gestured them into the room.

The agents consulted their card phones, sweeping them back and forth, scanning the room. One of the women stopped, her device pointing in his direction as she looked at him.

"The spirits are upset," Jamie raised his voice to be heard, "they don't like the technology that has entered the room. They want those people removed, or they won't go!"

The clergymen looked at him, then at the agents. Turning as one, they herded the agents back to the door, arms held wide, backing the agents away. Once at the doors, they ushered the people outside.

With a sigh of relief, Jamie nodded at the priests and smiled. "Much better," he said, "They have calmed, I can continue. But do not let them, or anyone, inside until I am done."

Hurrying, Jamie went through the motions of ceremony, pretending to release the unsettled dead souls that had caused the disturbances. After fifteen minutes, he announced the Cathedral to be cleansed. Assuring the Canons gathered around him, he asked for his payment and a quick route to a private exit where no one would see him leave. He was given both, the men wanting him to be gone as much as he wanted to be gone.

Slipping out a basement door, Jamie looked across the green and could see the huddled group of agents with their heads together. Sticking his hands in his pockets and hunching his shoulders, her turned the other way and wandered off, not rushing. Walk, he thought, people notice someone rushing. They don't notice someone just taking a walk.

Once he was a half dozen blocks away, looking over his shoulder every time he turned a corner to make sure he wasn't being followed, he hailed a cab. Sliding into the back seat he saw the Banksy graffiti, of the Well Hung Lover. He stared at it as the cabbie pulled into traffic.

A week later, Jamie sat in his home, stroking Zazzles, sipping a cuppa, and reading the dailies. The hauntings had returned to the

Bristol Cathedral. And The T.A.L.O.N. Agency was performing a full investigation.

It was too hot for him to return there. They would recognize him.

And though he wasn't sure if that female agent had actually detected what he had been doing or not, it wasn't worth the risk. It looked like some haunts couldn't be dispelled and the world would finally have definitive proof that things beyond explanation really did exist.

CASE 3456
CODENAME: EATER OF THE DEAD

She was being hunted. She ran.

She ran because they had labeled her a demon, a monster from the beyond who had possessed the body of their loved one. Their daughter, their sister, their wife, their mother.

It didn't matter what she was called. It didn't matter what she told them about why she changed, she was no longer what they had made her, and for that they would destroy what she had become.

When she first returned from the eternal abyss, as she had done so many times before, they were all amazed. Her mother and father cried, praising Krishna. Her children – the oldest already a father, and the youngest had her marriage arranged though she had not yet bled as a woman – had gathered close, wailing and praying, telling her that she had been gone from them for weeks. Her husband held her close, promising her a new dress and someone to help around the house, maybe have their oldest son and his wife move into their two bedroom house with their four kids.

She dodged around an oxen drawn cart, lifting her sari and her brown feet puffed on the dusty dirt trail between the squat stone buildings. A man on a moped zipped past, swearing as his tinny horn cut the air like an angry fly in your ear. Crowds of people bustled in the marketplace ahead, its canvas canopies snapping in the wind. She ran into the sooq, weaving between people. Dust clouded her vision and clogged her throat, the breeze became a sudden burst of air, toppling a small cart and knocking children off their feet.

Monsoon season would be here soon.

What an odd thing to think of at this moment.

She didn't even know how she knew that. But it was always that way, memories and knowledge popping into her head from previous lives. Some she had lived, but usually lives that others had lived. It was hard to separate the two. It was like waking from a dream and still being muddled from sleep. Or perhaps it was more like being asleep, but knowing you're dreaming.

A strain of another memory - one not from this life time, this body – came to her. A child's tune, a nursery rhyme, singing of row, row, row your boat.

She had been rowing though, upstream in a world that despised a woman using the oars. Her head railed against the thought of a boat, though another part of her was drawn to the sea by the memories of a dozen lives spent on waters where you could not see land.

The people of this land, her people in this life, accepted her new oddities after returning from her coma. They allowed her to buy books of maps, and even be a bit more in charge of life around her. It was when she said that everyone was old enough to cook for themselves that her family and friends began wondering about her. When she told them - without thinking first - that men were not superior to women only different, that a woman didn't need a man in her life, that was when her husband called for her father to come.

Her mother had tried to comfort her, telling her that the ideas were silly.

When she insisted and her mother couldn't convince her, her father and husband came in to beat her.

She'd fought back. That was the moment they realized she had been possessed. This was not the woman who had been hit in the head and slept for almost a month. This was some monster from beyond the grave, who came back to strike at those who loved and cared for her the most.

Angry cries from behind her spurred her feet to move faster.

A man in an American business suit ducked behind a stall in the bazaar, and a flash of fear passed across her memories. That was the outfit of a hunter also; the dark sunglasses, the hand under the dark jacket, the shiny shoes with thick rubber soles - all things the hunters in the world of cities wore when hunting her in other lives.

Everything was so muddled in her head. The feeling of running through the stalls, people stopping to stare, or reaching out to grab her sleeve and try to stop her, children running underfoot, goats scattering from her path was so similar to the feeling of the mix of thoughts in her head. It was chaotic, and no one understood that the noise was distracting and wouldn't let her finish her task.

She had one duty to perform and the tumult of life didn't even give her time to think it through and figure out what it was.

Her eyes stung from the grit and dust, sweat left rivulets of clean skin down her face and neck, and her feet ached from running across the stones of the square.

She saw him: one man in a clean white shirt opened to his belly button, a gold necklace catching the hot sun above.

The rest of his clothes were white also, pristine in the reality of the village. He was putting money into his wallet as he left a business.

A man stood in the doorway, wringing his hands, his wife and daughter behind him, holding one another and crying.

The man who had just left the building turned to his right, away from her, and swaggered towards a shiny silver car at the end of the alley.

This was the man who must die.

If she could do this task, then she could be at peace.

Running past one of the few remaining stalls before reaching a proper street again, the woman snatched a pole holding up the awning. The cloth fell atop the shouting proprietor, who stumbled out into the street, upsetting crates of fruit. The mob following her, a dozen men from her family, and a dozen more who joined in the chase, slowed for a moment but their voices raised up in frustration.

The man ahead stopped and turned to see what the commotion was, allowing her to close the last bit of distance. Her makeshift staff came down on the man's neck, where it met his shoulder, and he screamed and threw his arms up.

A sharp pain bit at the woman's backside, and her hand went to the spot automatically. She pulled a small dart from her well-padded behind and the world swayed around her, the ground threatening to leap up and meet her.

She stumbled, catching herself on the wall.

A glance behind showed two men in dark American business suits, with equally dark sunglasses, aiming their tranquilizer guns at her again.

The mob swelled past the shop and its fallen fruit, and the man in front of her found some bravery in her hesitation.

His angry face swam into her field of vision when she turned back to him. His hand reached for her, and she smacked it out of the way with the stick. His hand cracked and went limp, and a scream came from his mouth, though it was on the edge of her awareness.

One thought consumed her: he must die. It was imperative for others to live.

She jammed the stick into the man's throat, which crunched under the blunt end. Small chunks of dirt clung to his rough shaven neck and his cologne wafted past her nose. He smelled like a whore, not a man.

She jammed again and again, the man trying to fend her off, blood trickling from his mouth, his throat ruptured. Another stinging bite in her rump and the world swooned and spun, the tops of the square stone buildings replacing the end of the alley.

The mob surged forward, crowding into her field of vision, reaching for her. She was pulled upright and fists and feet hit her again and again.

The two men in suits watched. They frowned and shook their heads, one touching the arm of the other, and then they disappeared, turning away from the angry throng.

The last thing she saw was her father and husband, who loved her so much, battering her. Spit flew from their mouths as they cursed her. Anger transformed their faces, and hatred clouded their eyes.

The world whirled into black.

Its consciousness swirled in the miasma of the unconscious collective, at least that's the best it could figure out what to call where it was. Thrown around by tides of energy of what others would call the afterlife. It was like being caught in a cosmic tidal storm, thrown by waves and ebbs and flows of everything.

This was familiar and warm. There was no body to worry about; no hunger, pain, or urges irritate. There was no fear, hate, love, or expectation.

Everything was just there. It was as it should be.

Content was the closet word it could ever come up with to describe the feeling in a place where feelings were just a thread of an equation to true understanding. When most came here, they broke apart, blending and mixing with the everything. It was like pouring a cup of water into an ocean.

Or perhaps a drop of water.

A countless number of atoms from that one drop blending with something massive beyond comparison.

This is where the soul came after death. An ocean of everything and everyone. To be washed, cleansed, and sent back to experience more of life, only to return later and bring back the sustenance of learning and the nourishment that only knowledge can bring.

But it didn't break up and blend like the others that came. It was in the midst of the Source, but retained most of itself even when it returned to a body. Perhaps that is why it didn't get a new body each time it returned. Maybe that was why it didn't need those years of growing to understand how reality worked: how to walk, how to talk, how to interact with others.

It was not like a drop of water in the ocean, it was like a frozen nugget of hail – hard, frozen, protected - losing little of itself, and gaining little of the Source before returning.

It tried to move towards the center of the Source, but couldn't. The Source had no beginning and no end. It was everything and everywhere. There was no center, no point where it was stronger than anywhere else. It tried to release it conscious, to blend and become one with the surrounding energy. To not be individual; instead to be part of the whole.

That was when it was pushed out again, passing by an infinitesimal point of energy, picking up the essence of someone so it could become them enough to complete its mission.

"Earl," a woman said, affection lacing her voice, "you're never happy."

"They didn't salt their walk," his own voice sounded grainy and bitter, "it was covered with ice and snow. What kind of place does that?"

"Here, drink this," Mildred held a cup to his lips. He jerked his head back.

"Is it soda pop? You know I can't drink that crap."

"No, it's water."

"I guess I'll have to suffer with that then," he grunted, sipping from the plastic cup. Pulling away, he focused on the clean white room around him. Machines beeped, and a white curtain hung from the ceiling on silver beaded chains, a silver track set so it could be drawn out. The smell of pine cleaner and alcohol reached his nose. There was a tube in his arm, clear liquid flowing from a bag into him.

"Where the hell am I?"

"You had a fall, you're in the hospital," Mildred said. Her voice thickened with emotion, "I thought I lost you."

"Hospital? These damned people don't want nothing buy my money. And if it ain't them, then it's the insurance. Most of these people ain't even old enough to play doctor, let alone be one. We don't need to be here, and we wouldn't if those Mexicans knew how to salt the walk in front of their restaurant."

"Earl, you fell at home, on your own walk."

A middle aged man in a long white coat interrupted any reply, marched in, clipboard in hand.

"Well Mister Whitmire, looks like you're clear to go home. But let your wife drive, ok?" the doctor said.

"Well, look at you," Earl said, "you even been around long enough to remember Reagan being shot? The Space Shuttle Challenger? 9/11? I bet you never served your country, but you think you can just give orders to anyone because you got a clipboard and a lab coat."

"Yes sir, I remember all those things, and served six years in the Army," the doctor said with a smile. Turning to Mrs. Whitmire before the crotchety old man could answer, the doctor began giving release instructions.

"You ok, Earl?" Mildred asked.

"Yeah. Why you asking me that?" the old man patted her arm.

"You've just been different for the past few months. I guess the accident must've knocked some sense into you. You don't complain as much, and things don't upset you like they used to."

"Well, maybe I just came to realize how dear life is, and how good you are to me. That fall was like a wakeup call, Mildred. Something in me died that day, and it allowed something else to take its place."

Mildred nodded and set the stack of magazines and newspapers on the round wooden table next to Earl, moving his mason jar of sweet tea back. Sitting in the brocaded wing-back chair next to him, she reached for the remote. She hesitated.

"Earl, is it ok if I switch the channel, or are you still watching the news?"

"Of course, sweetie. You watch what you want; I can read the paper instead."

The woman watched the man she had married over forty-five years ago in wonder. He was a changed man, almost like a stranger. But she liked him, even with all the odd habits he'd picked up, like circling certain news articles or taking notes on his yellow legal pad about certain events.

He talked to people now too. Asked questions about them and their lives, and listened real careful. Even the foreigners. He never like them before, always saying they had a secret agenda. They wanted our jobs, our businesses, our women, or to just blow us up. But that was all different now.

Mildred smiled again, switching to her game shows, the familiar sound of the wheel ticking as it spun and the crowd cheering as it stopped. She rattled on about something that the women in the church group were working on, interrupting herself to guess the puzzle, and picking up where she left off as the contestant echoed her.

Earl thought he figured it out. He knew who had to be sent back. Well, anyone else would called it being killed, he thought he knew who had to be killed. The reasoning was fuzzy though. Not the reason it had to be done, it needed to be done.

But the reason he had begun looking for someone who had to die. It was either the minister, or the man who ran the local tobacco shop. Both were always nice, smiling and asking about your family. But neither liked to talk about themselves.

Earl knew though, knew that one of them would kill others through their actions. He wasn't sure when, but by the right man dying, thousands of others would live.

He loaded up the truck, crates of chemicals, gasoline, and set the fuse just outside the double windows of the cab.

With a sigh, he went inside to kiss Mildred goodbye for the last time. He would miss her. She was the high point of this trip. She had been married to a man who had been domineering and abusive for decades, and her eyes still shone with love for him.

Earl was glad he could give a few months of happiness with him, though she still flinched if he moved too quickly or suddenly. He couldn't feel guilty for that; it wasn't his doing. That was the old Earl.

Hiking up his loose blue jeans on his suspenders, he walked up the three steps of the porch and through the creaky screen door. It slammed shut behind up. The house smelled of Mildred's fresh biscuits, and he could hear her bustling about in the kitchen.

"Honey," Earl called from just inside the door, "I'm going into town to get a cigar from the tobacco shop. Roy wants to play cards tonight, and you know he always offers me a cigar. I thought I'd surprise him and bring one for him and me tonight."

Mildred came around the corner, slipping on a sweater, her purse in her hand.

"I thought you'd be going into town. I want to go with you."

"No," Earl said, a bit harsher than he meant to.

She flinched, her shoulders hunching instinctively from a blow that would have come from Earl before his accident. His heart ached; this poor woman had suffered so much, but still loved the man that had been her private monster. She only wanted to make him happy. He couldn't bring her though, she shouldn't be there today.

Not today.

"I'm sorry, Earl. I just thought I could go to the grocery and pick up some fixins for a roast. I was going to make your favorite, and we have so many biscuits that I need..." She trailed off, realizing that she had been talking back. She set her purse on the hall table and began to take off her sweater.

"Hey," Earl forced a smile onto his face, "it's ok. You can come along. Maybe you can go over and talk to Lois at the salon while I jaw with the guys at the tobacco shop. I'm gonna meet Greg there too."

"The minister visiting our church? He's such a nice man, and doing so much for the kids with his counseling," Mildred prattled on with a smile, putting her sweater on again and picking up her purse.

Earl shook his head. Greg watched Mohammed ring up the cigars, his eyes narrowed and suspicious of the smiling man behind the counter. Earl paid his eleven dollars and twenty-three cents, wondering when cigars got so expensive.

The wall behind the counter was filled with cartons of cigarettes, and the glass counters around the room showed ceramic pipes and other stuff used for recreational smoking.

Earl took his change, and told Greg to hold on while he went and put this stuff in the truck.

No one paid attention to the hunched old man making his way across the pot-hole filled parking lot to a beat up pickup truck. Now was the time to do it. Mildred was in the grocery and no one else was in the shop.

Getting in, he slammed the door and rummaged in the brown paper bag for a cigar. Pulling off the cellophane around it, he realized he didn't have anything to cut the end off with. Using his pocket knife, always kept sharp, he cut the tip off the cigar on the dashboard, swept the crumbled bits into his hand, and tossed them out the window. He laughed when he realized it wouldn't matter in a couple minutes.

He checked his pocket for the book of matches, lifting his butt from the seat, and pulled them out. Flipping back the cover, he stared at the twenty red match heads. He didn't have to do this. He could love Mildred and live out the rest of this life with her, dying when the time came. He thought he could.

Maybe it wasn't allowed. Maybe when he did die, they wouldn't send him back again, and instead let him come back new. How long had it been since he had been new? Five lives? Twenty? He couldn't remember. So many lives blended with others, and it was hard to tell them apart.

Mildred thought the confusion was just him getting old, but he knew better. A question, almost an urge, came to him with a powerful surge. Was a couple years of normal life worth the hundreds or thousands of lives that would be saved? No. The answer was no.

Earl lit a match and held it to the cigar, puffing. A small cloud of smoke formed in front of him. He pulled it out of his mouth, and looked at the end to see if it was completely lit. It took three more matches before it was, him spitting bits of tobacco out that got stuck to his tongue.

Starting the truck, he backed it out of the parking space so the back was facing the glass front of the store. Pulling on the cigar to get the cherry good and hot, he backed slowly towards the storefront. Stopping for a moment, he slid the glass doors apart so he could get to the fuse.

Looking around to check for traffic he saw a man in a black suit with dark sunglasses getting out of a plain back car. It was them, the hunters. How did they find him every time?

His time was almost up.

Slamming the truck into reverse, he moved his foot off the brake.

The agent in front of him drew a gun and fired two shots, small bursts sounding as the front tires exploded. The truck jerked and rolled backwards, much slower than he had hoped.

It might not be enough speed to shatter the glass in front of the store. The back tires popped onto the sidewalk.

The driver side door opened and another agent grabbed him by the shirt, pulling him half from the truck.

His foot slipped from the accelerator and the truck rocked to a halt, the flat front tires stopped by the curb. Fighting the man off, Earl leaned towards the passenger side of the cab, and saw Mildred running towards him, grocery bags swaying, a look of horror on her face. If this was going to be done, it needed to be before she reached the explosion area.

Earl grabbed the cigar from his mouth and turned to light the fuse, only to have the agent smack the cigar from his hand. It hit the floorboard, ashes and smalls coals scattering.

It was over, he couldn't fight this young man with his old body. The truck wouldn't have enough momentum to break the glass, and the cigar wouldn't have enough fire left to light the fuse. If he hadn't hesitated, thinking about Mildred and a life that could never be, then he would have succeeded.

The cigar receded as he was dragged from the cab of the truck, the agent pulling him to the ground. Grabbing at the doorframe, Earl pulled an old colt revolver from under the seat. Flopping to the ground he looked at the glass storefront in time to see both men inside run out of sight.

Mildred was coming around the truck when Earl put the gun under his chin and pulled the trigger.

The agent reacted a second too late.

It floated in the sea of the Source once more. It had failed that life, and thousands may have died because of it. The mote of energy sought information, moving in a place where movement was not an action, but rather a thought. Time was meaningless here and the past, present, and future all existed at once.

Yes, the information was there. The holy one had corrupted a young man who later built a device that killed hundreds. The shop owner had a son that finished educating himself and entered a trade of creating chemicals that killed millions.

To kill one to save thousands. It made sense when in life, just using logic. If you also added the emotion, it made even more sense. But did it make sense when not in life? If the Source collected experiences to gain knowledge and grow, then wouldn't the experience of thousands dying, and tens of thousands who were attached to them suffering the loss, be as valid an experience as those thousand living a long and full life? And who was to say one survivor may not go on to kill dozens of other people?

It collected more information, dodging about to nodes of energy without ever moving, researching all the people who survived.

Indeed, suffering was generated by one dying. Riots happened because of one death, hundreds injured, dozens dead, and people inspired to more violence. The family that the man in white had spoken to, giving them money for their daughter, had starved because the man had died. Their daughter had been saved from a life of slavery, but had died instead.

It paused, considering the ripple of long-term effects its actions had on the world. If the Source cherished free will, why would the Source give such missions? Did the Source even give these missions?

It couldn't remember being commanded, or asked. But the memories of human lives clouded the clean purity of this realm.

I am a killer, it thought.

The ripples of individualism spread outward in this place that didn't contain the dimensions of height, width, or depth. Is it my choice, my own free will, or do I do as the source commands? Am I a serial killer who only dies in body, but not spirit, coming back and using a righteous excuse? Can I say no to the Source, and do as I like?

It watched the energy of egoism and independence collided with the infinite expanse that was the Source.

The Source shuddered, and it was ejected from the warm confines of eternity and back into the limited reality of life.

The nurses scattered as Natalie sat up, calling for doctors. Natalie held on to that thread, that remnant of a dream, to the only thought this body had ever had.

The Source had shuddered.

She looked down at the simple yellow summer dress she wore, fingers caressing the material, fingers that had never flexed of their own accord. The muscles of this young child's body were atrophied, but still usable due to massage and physical therapy given by the staff in this facility.

Thoughts of her father entered her head: A journalist, a well-known one, that got special treatment from the hospital. He drank, and always smelled like booze when he came here. He made passes, and more, at the female staff. Even moving Natalie aside to use the bed when he had the urge to use it. He was a man drunk on petty power and tore people's lives apart with his whims and anger.

He should die.

But he loved her. He cared for her, even when his wife left. When this body, Natalie's body, had been a vegetable he still cared for her.

That was worth something right?

The knowledge of the place before, the Source, slid away. But Natalie knew she could make the choice. This mind was empty, so Natalie reached out, through the pinhole that led to the Source, and pulled information in. She filled this young mind with knowledge from far beyond human experience, and all her remaining knowledge of her past lifetimes. Dozens of lives filled her head. Sciences, philosophies, skills, all things she had learned through countless bodies flooded into her.

She gasped, her lungs drawing deeper than ever before. They stretched, weak muscles around them forcing them to take in extra oxygen.

The staff rushed back in, doctors checking her eyes, pulse, blood pressure.

"Excuse me please," Natalie moved one man in a white coat aside to reach for the remote control to the TV.

The men and women stared in amazement as a girl who had never moved on her own, let alone touched any electronic devices, turned on the news. The TV chattered in Danish about The T.A.L.O.N. Agency stopping a car bomber in the United States who tried to kill a Muslim man and a Baptist minister, labeling it a hate crime.

Natalie realized she had spoken in Hindi. She would have to be careful.

She let the staff go about their examination, leaning back and watching the news. She would protect this man who loved her, and she would watch out for any other karmic assassins that the Source sent. With the knowledge of how to fight them, she just needed to gain the strength. She could face down any command or attack the Source could send.

Through the pinhole, Natalie felt the Source shudder, and it felt pleased.

Travis I. Sivart

CASE 6843
CODENAME: VIGIL

"Middle-aged, black, single mom, but it still happened to me," Kim said to Tawana, pausing to take a drink of coffee they had picked up from a local roaster. "I have been embittered by life and the crap thrown at all of me for almost twenty years now, but it happened to me. I am still not even sure how it happened. It wasn't an explosion of chemicals and lightning, not a mutant critter attacking me, and definitely no aliens coming down to imbue me with gifts and responsibility. I had a fever, I remember that. Oh, it was a hellish one. I couldn't even take myself to the hospital, and my son kept bringing me water and cool towels. He was a godsend. He was always around, watching super hero movies, Star Wars, or Legos, or one of the half dozen scifi movie or TV franchises we share on a regular basis. Helped me get to the shower or bathroom, and kept me fed with Pop-Tarts and Chef Boyardee. I just laid there, shivering and dreaming, alternately burning up then freezing. My son kept close watch over me, did I say before how awesome my boy is?"

"You may have mentioned that," Tawana patted her friend's hand. "Go on."

"He never had it easy; I guess we both had it rough. I never really thought about it before, I just did what needed done. I got pregnant with Tyrone while trying to get a degree in community college. My boyfriend said it'd be ok, though, he'd take care of us. Four months later, he was gone. My mama said he would do it, and I don't think her nagging at him helped much. But I guess in the end, it was just

71

too much responsibility for him to handle. I never saw him again, and Tyrone never knew his daddy. Did I ever tell you that I named Tyrone after my daddy? My daddy died a hero, saving the lives of his boys in the Wall War of 27, so the two only met when Ty was just a baby. I wanted him to have a legacy of a strong, good, and honest man to follow.

"I did the best I could," Kim sipped from her cup, her eyes distant, "I had to drop out of college, still keep meaning to go back someday, but I guess that ain't gonna happen now. Not since my boy went missing. But I'll get to that.

"I couldn't afford a doctor when I was sick, but I went to the clinic after I had been sick a bit over a week. They couldn't find nothing wrong with me, not that they tried that hard. We waited for three hours before the doctor saw us, and then she only spent four minutes with us. I just wanted to make sure it wasn't contagious, that Tyrone wasn't going to get it. The doc said if he was going to get it, he would have already had it. She took blood, well, she sent a nurse to do that, then sent me home with a scrip for some anti-biotics."

"That clinic was funded by The T.A.L.O.N. Agency, and that was my first mistake. I never thought what would happen. They knew something, but they weren't telling anyone. Anyway, we went home and a few days later the fevers stopped. I still ached like no one's business, though. All my muscles felt like they had a Charlie horse, from my feet to my shoulders, and everything between. It was like a full body cramp, if my whole body was having its period.

"After that, it got better, though, everything eased up. I began losing weight and I was better than ever. I was quicker and could lift things that I couldn't before. Jars of peanut butter no longer were the challenge they had been. Of course, I lost my job waitressing because of the time I had been out. But I got a job at the grocery, ringing folks up."

"When did you begin to realize all the strange things though?" Tawana leaned forward across the diner table.

"Well, I told you about the jars being easier, but I didn't think a thing about it. It really made me wonder when I was picking up Tyrone from Taekwondo, and was watching him spar. The instructor, a big hunky brother that had been in the Mexican Border War, was sparring with one kid's dad who had kept up with his training, and I laughed when the guy took a punch from Mike, the black guy who ran the place.

"Mike asked me if I thought it was easy, flirting with me, I think. See, I had lost a lot of weight and was fitting into my old clothes. I had a halter top and yoga pants on, and I looked good, if you know what I mean. I told him I thought I could hold my own. He told me to come on out onto the mat.

"I kicked of my keds and strutted out there. Once there, I had no idea what I was doing. I asked him to show me some basics. So he squared up with the other dude and they went through some basic blocks and attacks, or whatever they called them. I watched them, then nodded and said I was ready.

"I think Mike took it easy on me at first, throwing punches that I easily slapped away, laughing at him. He surprised me and swept my legs out from under me. I went down on my back and it knocked the air out of me. He laughed and held out a hand to help me up, but I just glared at him, and flipped myself up onto my feet, just like in the movies. That was when shit got real.

"I went for him, even pacing, not crossing my feet like he showed me, throwing punches with a flat hand, just my knuckles curled under. He blocked them, but it was so easy for me! I kept going, and he was backing away. I laughed at him, thinking he was being nice. He tried that leg sweep thing again, and I leapt in the air, not even knowing what I was doing. I flipped girl, I did a goddamned flip, and brought my foot down on his neck, where it meets the shoulder, you know?

Tawana nodded, just holding her cup of forgotten coffee. "Then what? What happened after that?"

"I backed off, bouncing on the balls of my feet, waiting for him to get up. It took him a minute. He was on his hands and knees, shaking his head to clear it. When he did get up, he held his hands in front of him and told me that was enough. If we were going to do more, we'd need to pad up. I looked around, and the whole place was staring at me. Even Tyrone. It felt good to have my boy looking at me that way. I don't think he planned to sass talk me anymore after seeing that. Then Mike asked me where I trained!"

"Me, Tawana! I told him I hadn't trained anywhere, just what he showed me and what I saw in movies. He laughed and invited me back. I don't think he believed me."

"I wouldn't believe you, either."

"Well, I went home with Tyrone, he had homework and if I didn't get on him, he would wiggle out of it and watch the box instead. He was hooked on some cyber channel show right then, and spent every minute he could watching it. But I went back with him, every chance I could. I took him twice a week, but couldn't stay every time. But when I did, wow, I learned quick. Within two weeks, Mike couldn't lay a hand on me."

"So what happened after that?" Tawana asked. "Not with the dojo, but with the other stuff."

"Ok, I got a call from the clinic. They said I needed to come in for a follow up visit. I told them I felt fine and didn't need to; after all, it had been a month. They said I needed to, and they wanted Tyrone there, too, to make sure he didn't get it. We both went in and they drew blood again, but lots more of it and from both of us. Oh, and we didn't have to wait at all. They showed us back to a room the minute we walked through the door. And the doctor stayed with us the whole time, asking lots of questions. Things about family history, and that sort of thing. They did a full physical on both of us. I was worried; I thought maybe I had something horrible. They even did a hand scan of me, you know with those hand-held MRI things?"

Tawana nodded.

"Anyway, they sent us off, saying we were fine but to come back if I noticed anything strange or different. So, I did what anyone would have done, I shut up, didn't tell them anything else, and decided I wouldn't be going back there f my life depended on it!"

"I don't blame you, you know when they do all that they want something from you, and they ain't gonna tell you what it is." Tawanna gripped her mug tighter.

"Amen, don't I know it! But I felt great. You know what else?"

Tawana shook her head.

"I was starting to squint, especially at night, and thought I would need glasses soon. Maybe just for driving and reading, so two sets of glasses. But I didn't anymore. My eyes just fixed themselves. I could see like an owl at night. I could hear better. When Tyrone was in his room, sneaking his game after bedtime, I could hear him hitting the screen pad, and I could hear the sound from his ear buds, even from the kitchen. I mean, not if I was running the water and doing dishes, but any other time. It was wild. He was a bit freaked out, I think, wondering how I knew. I just told him it was 'Mom powers'.

"I was a new woman. It showed at work, too. When I took down some punk trying to shoplift with a simple wrist lock, a guy who saw it asked if I had ever done security. I told him no, and he asked me if I would like to. He said he'd train me and everything. Two weeks later, I had gone through training, top of my class, and even trained in firearms."

"You use guns now?" Tawana asked.

"Yeah, I'm good at it, too. Never miss what I aim for, and the kick ain't nothing. They worked with me on my schedule, because I had a kid. I couldn't just work and not be there for Tyrone. But Kyle, that's the guy that ran Schindler's Security Specialists, put me in special jobs. I'd be the one who guarded the famous musician or actor who came to town. They even had me trailing a Senator on back-up security. I was watching his security dudes, to make sure they didn't fuck. Now, you know I didn't have enough for a magnacar of my own – I just used the train or bus or whatever - but they just gave me one. Sent me through a special stunt-driving class and everything.

"Everything seemed to be looking up, I even started taking classes on the net again, to finish my degree. I had some savings set aside, and even helping Tyrone with his homework was easy now."

"So what happened to you? What made all this stuff happen?" Tawanna was almost climbing over the table.

"I don't know. No idea. Like I said before, I was me, then I got sick, then I was… super me! But then I came home one day, and there was a social worker there. She said Tyrone had been taken away because he showed some kind of infection in his blood. The clinic had told them about it. She said he was ok, but I couldn't see him for a few weeks. I could call him, but I wouldn't be allowed to visit him. She said the school confirmed that he had been acting weird at school, aggressive and despondent. I don't know what the hell they were talking about! The school hadn't said anything to me. When I went to talk to the principal, he said that it was all true. When I asked to talk to the teachers, he said I couldn't. They were all too scared, he said. What the hell?"

"Yeah, that's some bullshit there. I would have kicked down some doors and made them talk to me."

"I couldn't. The principal had security in the room with us, and I couldn't do anything, because they'd arrest me. I had to be around for when Tyrone got out of wherever they took him to."

Tawana patted Kim's hand again as the woman quieted and swallowed, visibly upset.

The waitress came over, refilling their coffees and asking if they wanted pie.

They both said yes, and the woman left.

"They took him, Tawana." Kim's voice cracked and she fell silent.

The waitress brought the pie with extra forks, smiling at the two women. When neither responded the waitress left without a word.

"I know," Tawana rubbed her friend's forearm. "But you're gonna get him back."

"I know I am," Kim sounded resolute and driven, her voice a spike of steel. "I am going to get him back, and that's why I called you here. I couldn't talk about this at my place. I think it's being watched. All that security training taught me a few things, and made me watch for things I would have never even thought to look for before.

"No, let me talk," Kim stopped the other woman from speaking with a look and gesture. "I don't know where they took Tyrone. I have no idea if it's a hospital or a home, or what. I just know I am going to find him. You know they told me he was dead?"

"What?" Tawana gasped. "No, you didn't tell me that!"

"That's because I think they're lying. I also think they're coming for me. Kyle let me go. Said he had to, for reasons he couldn't explain. Then he said something weird. He said I could keep all the gear, and even the car until I get my own. Said he would pay me a good severance package, and that I should be really, really careful. He actually used the word 'very' twice. He looked sad to let me go, like he wanted to do more, but was afraid.

"The world has changed. I don't mean from when I was a kid, I mean from a month or two ago. I see so much more now."

"Kim, you sound crazy right now. Do you hear yourself?" Tawana gripped one of the forks.

"Yeah, I know how crazy I sound. But I also know that things don't make sense unless you look at it in a certain way. That's why I called you. I needed to tell someone. Someone who could get the story out there if I don't come back."

"What?" Tawana pulled her hand back, dropping the fork, leaning back in the booth. "I am not some reporter, or even a government agent. Not anymore."

"I know, but you were military, and you have a clue what folks are doing. You worked security, and you know a few people. There is something damn wrong going on, and I am going to find out where my son is. Even if it kills me."

Tawana looked at Kim, giving her a scared look.

"I know, I hope it doesn't but it's my boy. I will do whatever I need to do to make sure he's ok. And if he is alive, which I know he is, then he is better out here than locked in some room with doctors poking him with needles. I think they think he has what I got, and that he will be a tool they can use. I won't let that happen. I don't know what they're doing to him right now, but I am going to find him, and save him from whatever they plan to do to him. I just pray to God that it isn't too late!"

"Kim, listen to me. You can't take on the government."

"The T.A.L.O.N. Agency ain't the government."

"No, they ain't. But they have enough money to make people do what they want, without the restrictions the government has to follow. They're more dangerous! What can you do against them? And why would they lie to you about Tyrone anyway?"

"I have certain gifts and skills now. I don't know how or why I got them. I don't know if they infected me with something, or if God himself reached own and touched me. But I do know that I'm not the same woman who loved without thinking only to be walked all over by men all my life. I ain't the scared little girl who dropped her chin whenever my mama looked at me with hatred eyes and vinegar in her voice. I am more now, and I have learned a few things I haven't told you. I can't tell you." Kim took a manila envelope from her messenger bag on the bench beside her and slid it across the table to Tawana. "This is what I have already told you, with names and addresses. It has some money in there, too. No, don't try and refuse it. You may need it to pay folks to listen, or to get out of town. I am putting you in danger just by being in public with you, but I thought it was safer than meeting you in private, where 'they' could do something without anyone seeing. I will send you more information, and I will do it in large white envelopes that look like insurance papers or medical papers, just so no one thinks anything of it. You need to listen to me now, I ain't never been crazy, and though I sound it right now, I am still pretty damn sane. I am just acting crazy because they took my boy. People don't do that. They don't tell a mother that her son was accidently cremated before she saw the body, then tell her it was for medical infection reasons. People don't do that."

"Ok Kim," Tawana took her friend's hand again and squeezed it tight. "I believe you. I am here for you. I see things too, everyone does. But we all don't say anything, because it's too dangerous if what we think turns out to be true. What will you do next?"

"I will bring down the heavens, and spread hell on earth to rescue my boy. I will be a shadow when I need to be, and a wildfire when I don't. I'll find Tyrone, and we'll be together again. And ain't no one on God's green earth gonna stand in my way once I set my mind to something."

"Don't I know that's the truth. Ok, go find your boy, but be careful, and I will be here once you get done."

"Tyrone?" Doctor Walters asked again. "Did you understand the question?"

"Yes," the boy looked around the sterile room while holding down his paper gown.

"Go ahead and answer it then," the doctor adjusted his thick black-framed glasses on his broad nose.

"Why do you use a clipboard instead of a tablet?" Tyrone glanced at the clipboard clutched to the doctor's chest.

"Because I like it better, and can review the information before entering it in the computer later, and make sure it is all correct. I don't like to add extra stuff that others don't need to know. Now, how about answering my question. Was your mother ever sick like this before?"

"Is it because I'm black? I heard that people used to do things to others, experiment on them because they were black."

"No, Tyrone," Doctor Walters laughed, "I'm black too, and we are here to help you."

"No sir," Tyrone mumbled, "she wasn't ever sick like this before. When is she gonna be better? When can I see her?"

"We don't know that, Tyrone." Walters shifted his pen from his lip to his pocket, and pulled his clipboard in front of him, studying it and not looking at the boy. "But we did find some of the genetic tracers in you that your mother had. So, your life could be in danger if this isn't handled properly. We want to start you on a program to help alleviate symptoms and control the situation. It would mean hard work, and you'd have to listen to what you're told. But with exercise and a strict training regimen, you can life a long life, even with your condition. Can you do that?"

The men behind the glass leaned together, keeping their voices down even though the observation window was thick enough to block any sound, so they could hear each other over the speaker.

"The man is a complete idiot," Agent Michaels sneered, "and we'll be lucky if he doesn't ruin this. If that kid was already a teenager, he'd probably see right through this bumbling fool."

"He may just be sympathetic," Specialist Westbrook suggested. "We will have to observe him. Have our agents found the mother yet?"

"She's disappeared; we have trackers watching probable targets of interests she may turn up at, though."

"As long as we keep an eye on this boy, he is the key to a potential gene link to a new super soldier. But send out hunters for his mother. If she has gone to ground, then she is a threat. And bring Doctor Patel in on this case, just in case Walters is a risk."

Kim sat in the Net Café, her coffee growing cold next to her basket of fish and chips. She set down the bar computer and unrolled the screen, which stiffened with the electric and magnetic field, and the keyboard projected onto the table. The fifteen centimeter long, one centimeter tall, and three centimeter wide computer was expensive, but worth it because of portability. It linked to her card phone, so both held the information she needed, but this was easier to use. It connected to the LiFi instantly. She looked around the room; no one paid her any attention.

She tapped on the lightboard, and typed in her search, the locations of local T.A.L.O.N. Agency popping up on the screen. She searched for her son's name and nothing came up other than the usual trash that comes up in any search. Nothing related to her son. No news stories, nothing except unrelated crap. She would need to access their computer system.

Picking up her mug, she leaned back with a sigh. She was a working mother, not some secret agent who could hack into a system like in the movies. She wouldn't even know where to look if she could get into an Agency computer. Not to mention, the security features of fingerprint or retina scans, let alone if they had the new DNA recognition programs that were being used. She didn't have connections to help her, and even if she could find someone, she didn't have the money needed to bribe or pay them.

And then there was figuring out who she could trust.

What was her next step? How did she find her son?

She stared at the screen, mentally noting the local offices of the Agency. Three stood out. One was a field office for their security, one was the medical research center outside of the city, and the last was a recruitment center for agents.

Frustration welled up inside her, tears coming to her eyes. She had to find her boy!

She brought the lukewarm coffee to her mouth, breathing in the smell. She stopped, and sniffed again: the bitter liquid had a sweet undertone. She hadn't ordered any flavor or sweetener.

Looking around again, no one was looking at her. They were all looking anywhere *but* at her.

A quick peek to the counter showed standard employees taking orders, and a manager leaning against the door frame to the back. He looked down when she looked at him.

With a glance her way, he dropped his eyes again and turned away, going into the back.

She wasn't safe here. Or was that paranoia?

It wasn't worth the risk. She pressed the power button on her computer and the screen went limp. She rolled it around the base, and tucked it into a pocket of her cargo pants, standing. Wrapping the fish and chips in the wax paper inside the basket, she headed for the door, taking a bit of the flounder.

Her jacket flew open when she exited the restaurant, the wind grabbing it, exposing her weapon to a strolling couple.

The man pulled the woman closer, and they walked a wide circle around Kim, nodding. Kim smiled, knowing the security badge showed also, and the couple would probably think she was law enforcement.

Glancing over her shoulder, she saw the manager on the phone, speaking animatedly and watching her. They were tracking her. That, she could handle.

She walked to her car, making sure she didn't rush. People noticed when someone rushed. The car unlocked when she approached and with a single command the electric engine hummed to life, the charging foot rising from the plate in the parking space into its storage compartment. Cardphone syncing with the interior GPS, directions to the three destinations appeared on the windshield corner readout.

On a whim she swiped them from the screen and took the wheel, merging with traffic when the directional light showed the way was clear. She knew where she was going and didn't need the net help. Besides, companies logged when you went anywhere, dates, times, and every other bit of information they could get. Kim had turned it off, having learned how to do that in her security training, but the city cams still tracked everything, registering VIN numbers from chips inside a passing car. And ever since the big three mobile companies merged under T.A.L.O.N., Inc. it had been worse. Services were more interconnected than ever before, but so were the subtle intrusions that people allowed into their lives, all in trade for convenience.

"Kiki phone," Kim ordered. Her phone lit up, recognizing her voice and ready for commands. "Run Kim Deletion Program Seven, prepare to initiate recovery identity, Vigil."

"Of course, Kim," said a smooth female voice from the car speakers. "Shall I record the changes with your provider, local law enforcement, and other interested agencies? If I do so, you will receive coupons and offers in the value of seven hundred and fifty dollars and a free updated ID card with full chip integration for home, mobile, and work."

"No, reconfigure all data transmission to one way only, and take the car offline also."

"Understood, Kim. I am required to tell you that such actions are not recommended and may lead to missing important and valuable information and offers in the future. Do you want to continue?"

"Yeah, continue. Do what I told you, damn it."

"OK, Kim, beginning program," the computer voice said. After a brief pause, a deep male voice spoke, "Welcome Vigil, and I hope you're happy with the changes you have made. I am your new construct, per your request. What shall you call me?"

"Kiki is fine, mister. And change the level from professional interaction to casual with twenty-percent ego reinforcement."

"You got it, beautiful. Just let me know what you need, and I am here for you anytime you need, for anything you want."

"Thanks, Kiki."

"My pleasure, Vigil," the suave masculine voice purred, bringing a smile to Vigil's face.

It was done. Though she didn't have the skill to do it herself, she had run across a guy while on security detail that could. Kyle had left the program in the glove box on a travel hub, and though Vigil didn't know why he had, she was grateful.

"Kiki, control the wheel and take me to the free clinic. I have to rearrange a few things then will take the wheel back."

"You got it, babe. Remember I only keep you on track where the sensors are installed. If we go outside their range, I'll let you know to take the wheel back if you haven't already. You want any music?"

"Yeah," Vigil said, "put on my angry mix, I need something to get me psyched up for what comes next."

Heavy bass bumped the speakers, electronic synth behind it. A man and woman went back and forth about how life will get you if you don't get it first.

Vigil pulled a black duffel from the back, popping the back seat up to get it from the storage compartment. Shuffling through it, she strapped her gear on. Taking the wheel back from Kiki, she tapped the wheel to the beat while making her way to begin a career outside of the law.

Vigil was hunting now. She had left the car five blocks away, parked in a movie theater parking lot and walked here, watching for tails. From her earbud, Kiki fed her information about local police activity as she crouched in the chill autumn air beside the building across the street from the free clinic. There were some changes since she was last here.

The familiar TA logo, a capital T superimposed over a capital A, of The T.A.L.O.N. Agency had been placed outside, to the left of the doors, and a few other minor cosmetic changes were obvious. Vigil wondered what other changes they had made. It didn't matter, she would do whatever was needed to find Tyrone, and no one - and no thing - would stand in her way.

After watching the building for thirty minutes she decided that everyone had gone home for the night. She could disable the alarm, and then it was just a matter of figuring out how to access the computer system. That was a slim hope, but she would never give up the hope of rescuing her child.

Looking both ways, Vigil tucked her hands in her jacket pockets and crossed the cycle aisle and street, head down but eyes scanning forward.

She stepped onto the sidewalk directly in front of the doors, but turned to the right and wandered down the street. Stopping at the corner, she checked her jacket and pants pockets, searching for something, and looking around. Scanning building roofs, down each direction of the four-lane city streets. Traffic zipped past, humming quietly with their electric engines, the smell of ozone wafting on the breeze.

Feigning disgust and shrugging, she turned back the way she came and walked past the clinic again to the next street corner. Repeating the process, she appeared to find whatever she had been searching for, patting her inside pocket with a smile, and turned back towards the clinic once again.

She slid into the shadows of the buildings, gliding across the alley beside the office. The doors were set in a small alcove, squared pillars with the TA logo on each side, and three steps leading up. Slipping into the well-lit recess, she dipped into a pouch on her military-style web belt, drawing out an electronic pad scrambler and a set of old-fashioned lock picks. She gave a casual glance around - pretending to choose music on her cardphone - and she placed the scrambler on the keypad to the right of the door. When the red and green light flashed alternately, she stepped to the physical lock to open it.

"Freeze!" a commanding voice came from the alley to the left of the niche Vigil was in. "T.A.L.O.N. Security, you are trespassing on private property. Stand down or prepare to be restrained and detained!"

Crap, it's a setup! Vigil spun to face the voice. Her eyes adjusted to the dark of the side street with a couple blinks and six men came into sharp focus. The one who had spoken and three others, in riot gear;

rifles in hand, smoke and shock grenades on belt, stun baton in hip holster, plasteel armor, and full face helmets. One man stood a dozen feet behind the others, dressed in a straight-cut suit, jacket, gray and black striped tie, and tinted glasses that screamed of tech. He watched her with crossed arms and feet apart at shoulder width, studying her with no expression.

At the sound of weapons being cocked, Vigil spun into action, throwing her body towards the now-empty street in a twirl to throw off their shots, while tossing an electro-ring towards them.

Rounds ricocheted off the sidewalk and street as she fell into a crouch. The stun device flashed and the electrical device threw out the field that would knock out anyone in a three-meter circle. The static charge was absorbed into the men's dampening devices on their belts and their visors went dark for a moment, protecting their eyes from most of the light.

Leaping forward to engage them before they could recover, the sound of another round sounded to her right, on the other side of the clinic entrance, and a sharp burst of pain blossomed in her ribcage. She crumpled to the ground from the force of the impact, but her body armor stopped the round from doing more than bruising her ribs.

Stupid! Didn't check your corners, good way to get yourself killed. She drew the pistol on her left thigh at the same time snatching the other from her shoulder holster with her right hand. Still prone, she fired towards the single shooter with her right, and towards the other men with her left. Her rounds ripped into the men's chests, their armor absorbing the shots. Time slowed; she heaved her body up, sliding her legs under her while keeping her targets in her sights.

She didn't want to kill, just disable, but the armor would make that almost impossible.

Rifles swung towards her.

She squeezed the trigger in her right hand and the lone gunman by the door went down, his head snapping back. She pushed herself forward and to the left, bringing her inside of the lead agent's rifle, her elbow cracking his visor, his head slamming into the alley wall behind him. Her left leg swept out and her boot connected with the throat of another man in riot gear.

Three down, three to go.

The two remaining in riot gear had a bead on her now.

She leapt up, towards the men, their barrels following her path.

Two blasts took her in the chest, throwing her upper body back, but her ankles wrapped around the neck of her target. She twisted, going down, a popping noise sounding from her enemy's neck.

The remaining man in heavy gear stood, firing four shots into her belly.

Her breath whooshed out, and gasping she lashed out with a foot, connecting with his knee.

The man went down, his knee bent backwards.

The remaining agent in the suit drew a pistol from his shoulder holster under his jacket.

Vigil flipped to her feet, still unable to breathe, and smacked the gun from his hand with her pistol.

The man fell into a barehanded fighting stance, but was slow. Her gun-laden hands landed a blow on his solar plexus, his throat, and his face before he could throw a single punch.

The agent crumbled to the asphalt in front of her.

Vigil stood still, trying to gasp air. Black spots swam before her eyes, the men laying still around her or moaning in impotent pain. Her midsection throbbed and she held it, warm liquid spread under her fingers. Air came to her in slow wheezes, her throat aching from the effort.

Regaining her senses, she saw the man with the shattered knee crawling for his gun. In two steps she reached him and tore off his helmet. A single punch put him out of the running. Seeing the agent in the suit stirring, she grabbed him by the collar and dragged him to the door. She dropped him beside her, putting a boot on his neck as she completed picking the lock.

"Thirty seconds," the agent under her foot mumbled. "You took out six fully trained men in full riot gear in thirty seconds."

"Yup," Vigil sneered at the man, "and in three minutes or less you're going to help me locate my son."

"No way that's happening," the man spat.

"I didn't say you'd have to be awake to do it," Vigil slammed her fist against the side of his head, knocking him unconscious.

The door opened and Vigil limped inside, one hand on her ribs, the other dragging the agent. Rounding the reception desk, she keyed the computer to life. The hand scanner lit up, as did the retinal scanner.

"They've upgraded this, too, since I was last here. Well agent, you're up."

Vigil lifted the man's hand to the scanner, and linking an arm under his, lifted his face to the retina scanner. Pressing her body against his, propping his body up between her and the edge of the desk, she reached up with the arm holding him and pried his eyelid open. The computer screen blinked and lit up with the interface ready.

Twenty miles away from the clinic, Vigil went over the information about Tyrone she had downloaded to her cardphone while wrapping her ribs. The wounds weren't too bad, at least not as bad as she had thought. Her body armor had taken the brunt of it, but a few direct shots at point blank was more than most armors could handle. Gritting her teeth, she bound the bandages tighter. Kiki repeated the information in his deep baritone, while she took care of her injuries. The facility that held Tyrone was just a couple hours away. She had thought it would be the closest one, but for some reason they had taken him farther away. She did find information on her son in the computer, and Kiki told her all about the genetic anomalies and matches between her and her son.

Vigil checked into the hotel under an alias, using cash – not something many places accepted anymore since the restructuring of the markets – and used faked identification. The computer and the clerk had both given her the most cursory once over before everything went through. The name she had adopted, Vigil, wouldn't just be something she used for an alias. She had gone too far, and there wouldn't be any going back. She was running now, and relying on the skills she had learned as security. Defending herself against the men outside the clinic wouldn't be something she could just walk away from. She would be hunted now.

The hotel she had chosen was one of the new kind that the entrepreneurs of the U.S. copied from the Japanese and Chinese. Her room was no larger than a walk in closet with a window at the opposite end from the door. Drawers lined the space under the bed, the TV recessed into the wall above the foot of the bed. Across from the top half of the bed, the desk held the full array of net needs and charging ports. A shower and toilet with a short ceramic counter with a mirror on the wall above were combined into one small room beside the desk. Built for efficiency rather than comfort, hotels could fit three to four times as many rooms into the same space. Even if they cut their prices in half, they still multiplied their profits.

Her armor was trashed. She would have to get another set of underarmor and a lined jacket before setting off to get her son. The gear she had taken from the men outside the clinic, could as a disguise. She knew of a few places downtown where she could get such things, but the chances of being seen on a city surveillance camera was too risky. Using one of her aliases, she logged into Amazon and ordered what she needed. It would be dropped via delivery drone within three hours, and the front desk would notify her when it arrived.

Money would be an issue, but she thought she had a handle on that. Living in the slums most of her life, she knew there were people who made money off of other's suffering. They usually had cash or untraceable, throw-away credit cards, not to mention a supply of weapons, vehicles, and armor that wouldn't have serial numbers. Enough that she could use it and stay under the radar.

But Tyrone came first. The big question was what to do once she got him. She couldn't drop him with family or Kim, not without him being picked right back up. The only option she could see was to keep him with her. That would mean educating him herself. Her friend, Dawn was in Regina, Canada, and that was one possibility, close enough to Chicago. Maybe leaving the country was the way to go. Well, she would handle that if – no, when - she got him back.

The cardphone singing woke her. It was the front desk letting her know her package had arrived. She went down and got it and came back upstairs. She fell asleep flexing the armor to get the new-set stiffness out.

She woke again to the afternoon sun streaming in the tinted windows. Stretching, her side twinged. It didn't hurt as much as she had thought it should. Frowning, she unwrapped her bandages. The wound was well-scabbed, and some parts were even flaking and showing new, pink skin beneath.

This was new, but it aligned with all the other stuff: heightened strength, speed, vision, hearing, dexterity, and more. Now her immune system was boosted, and her healing accelerated. With a grim smile - and an idle thought of what the hell happened to make her this way – she poked her cardphone and brought Kiki to life, directing him to give her more information about The T.A.L.O.N. Agency. News reports, press releases, whatever could be found. Any information was one more thing she could use once she set out for her assault and rescue of her boy.

Three days later Vigil was fully healed and in her magnacar, riding the electric rails towards the city line, heading to the research facility. She shook her head; there was no way she was ready to do this, but delaying wouldn't help. The sooner she got there, the more likely she was to succeed.

Kiki warned her that T.A.L.O.N. was still on full alert, that they were expecting trouble. She only hoped the four days she had spent in hiding made them overconfident and not expecting her yet.

She had debated the best time to enter the facility, day or night. Night guaranteed less personnel inside, but it also meant more closed off sections and higher security. She wasn't a tech geek, to use the term from her childhood, so hacking through systems and doors wasn't her strong suit. And without the right equipment, it would have to be a daytime entry. Her gear couldn't be hidden, but there was little she could do about that. She had planned her escape as best as she could, the exit strategy was the most important part, and relied as much on luck as it did any plan on her part.

Parking the car in the employee parking lot - avoiding the parking garage, knowing it would be closer once she escaped, but harder to get out of – she slipped on the last of her gear and the jacket and other scavenged items from the last fight at the clinic. She looked close enough to the agents she fought, sans the helmet and rifle, that she would pass a cursory inspection.

Getting in was easy, and entering through the service entrance brought little problems. One of the security guys even held the door open for her. Chivalry, and stupidity, wasn't dead. Thank goodness for small favors.

She smiled and nodded at passing people, making her way by memory to the medical wing. Stopping at the admissions desk, she checked in at the sign in tablet, using the ID lifted from the fight, and headed deeper into the belly of the beast. She knew Tyrone's room number, at least what it was four days ago. No guarantee he was in it; he might be out of his room for testing or whatever else they had him doing. It was after dinner, so she hoped he was in his room and not in a common room. Just to be sure she passed through the cafeteria and rec room. Pausing, she looked around. No one else was dressed like her in this part of the center, and she stood out. Most didn't pay her much attention, but one doctor noticed and made a beeline for her.

Looking down and stuffing her hands in her pockets, Vigil exited and headed towards the hall where Tyrone should be housed.

"Pardon me, miss?" an accented voice - it sounded Indian - spoke from behind her. "Excuse me, you in the black. Ma'am?"

The first real test. Vigil sighed, turning towards the man.

"Yes," she said, glancing at his name tag, "Doctor Patel? What can I do for you?"

"What are you doing in this section? Do you have clearance?"

"Of course, Doctor. Why else would I be here? I'm doing a routine security check, and then it's time for my lunch break. Is there a problem you need to report?"

"Can I see your ID?" Doctor Patel ignored her question.

"Of course, can we step out of the hallway to do this? I wouldn't want to alarm anyone, and checking my ID could cause some apprehension among the staff."

"Yes, let's go to my office where I can call this in."

"How about we just step in here?" Vigil grabbed the man by his arm with one hand and his badge with the other. Scanning the ID on the pad outside a supply room, she pushed the door open with her foot and shoved him inside. Glancing down the hall, Vigil made sure no one was looking before following the doctor in and shutting the door behind her.

The man stood with his hands up in front of him, and smiled.

"Just wait a second," Patel said, "don't do anything rash. We can talk about this."

"Communication hasn't been the Agency's strong point so far." Her fist flew out and connected with his jaw. Grabbing him by his lab coat, she pulled him towards her, swinging his back against her and wrapping an arm around his neck. Tightening her grip, she cut off his air supply. "Go to sleep Doctor, that way I don't have to hurt you."

The man struggled, digging his fingers into her armored jacket, struggling to speak. She held him as easily as she would a child, kicking his feet out from under him so he couldn't push her backwards against the door and alert anyone passing by. His feet kicked as he gurgled and gasped; now clawing in desperation to get a breath.

"Fucking sleep, asshole." Vigil growled, "Take my son from me, will you? I will do whatever is needed to get him back. Including killing your sorry ass, so fucking sleep before I need to snap your damned scrawny pencil-pushing neck!"

The man went limp in her arms. She held him for fifteen seconds more before lowering his body to the ground. Checking his pulse, she made sure he was alive. She hesitated for moment, not sure if that was the best option. He would have a bad headache, but would live.

With a sigh to settle her nerves, she snatched his ID badge from his pocket and tucked it in hers. She took his wallet, cardphone, and his floor schedule, then rolled him under the metal shelves. Unfolding the sheet, she checked the room assignments. The assholes hadn't even moved Tyrone; he was still in the same room. Either that meant they were over confident, or it was a trap. Well, either way, she was going to get her boy.

Grabbing some sheets and pillow cases, she cracked the door and looked into the hall. A nurse stared at her, and with a smile, Vigil stepped out. Waving at the woman, Vigil turned towards Tyrone's room and let the door close on its own, fighting the urge to force it to close faster so no one would see what had happened inside. Walking at a casual pace, she left the supply room behind.

Three turns later, she approached the room assigned to her son. Stepping to the door, she looked through the small window. A man in a suit stood with his back to the door, and Tyrone sat on the bed staring past him, straight at her. Her son's eyes went wide and she turned away, pressing her back to the wall beside the door. An orderly pushing a patient in a wheelchair looked at her, his eyebrows raising.

"Sponge bath," she whispered with a nervous smile, looking at the man going past her. The orderly exhaled a single breathy laugh and continued on.

Peeking back into the room, the man in the suit turned back to her son. Tyrone looked at her again and she held a finger to her lips, motioning him to be quiet and look away. The boy was good at listening to his mother, and did as she indicated. She reached for the handle, opening the door and slipping inside.

The man had a hand in a pocket, and turned to look at her, surprise barely registering on his face.

"Good evening," the man in the suit said in a familiar way, "a pleasure to have you here. I am Specialist Westbrook, and we thought you might be on your way."

Throwing the sheets at the agent, Vigil burst into action, fist flying towards him.

The agent batted the linen away with one hand and knocked her blow with away with the other. His hands shot out, his fingers curled under and heading for her throat.

She leaned back, out of his reach, and his punch fell inches short of cutting off her air supply. Punches flew, each of them parrying the other's with little effort.

He was as fast as her!

Tyrone crabbed backwards on the bed and into the corner. A flurry of attacks filled the room, both combatants testing the other and trying to score a hit. Each fought with skill, using hands, feet, and full body attacks to gain the advantage.

"You should give up," Specialist Westbrook said, "I sent an alarm the moment I saw you from my cardphone. Others will be here any moment. Don't endanger your son with further foolishness."

Vigil renewed her attack, enraged at the thought of failing now. Westbrook was hard pressed to keep up with her assault, and Vigil connected with three different blows. One to the solar plexus knocked the air from the man and bent him forward; another to the chin snapped his head back and threw his arms wide; and the third, a kick to the chest, threw him back against the window blinds with a crash. His coat flew back; he had a weapon.

Recovering, Specialist Westbrook reached into his coat after it.

Sliding the cuff of her jacket back and dropping her fist down, Vigil launched three needle-sized darts from a metal bracer on her wrist.

The needles embedded in the man's neck and face, and his eyes widened and his body stiffened. He fell, his face as frozen as the rest of his body.

Reaching down, Vigil recovered the agent's weapon, cardphone, and ID badge. She jammed the first item into the back of her waistband and pulled the jacket over it, and the other two items went into pockets.

"Baby," she said, turning to her son, "you ok? Tyrone, are you alright, sweetie?"

The boy's eyes registered his mother, and the shock and fear slid from his face. He threw himself off the bed, crashing into her arms for a hug. Holding her tight, Tyrone looked up at her with a wide smile.

"You were awesome! Can you show me how to do that? That guy said I got the same thing you do, but he called it a sickness. So can I do that stuff too?"

"OK baby, calm down. One thing at a time. First we gotta get outta here, ok?"

Tyrone nodded and glanced at the door.

Vigil shook his shoulders. "Stay behind me, but stay close. If I gotta fight again, stay close but get against a wall or in a corner ok? Stay between me and anyone else coming at us, ok? Do you understand, Tyrone?" She shook him again.

The boy nodded again, looking from the paralyzed agent to the door. He watched his mother checked the hall through the small window in the door, making sure the noise hadn't drawn any attention.

Opening the door, she put one hand on Tyrone's shoulder and guided him into the hall. They turned away from the direction she had come in and walked with a calm and even pace towards the end of the hall and the stairwell.

She held Tyrone with a firm grip, and he kept pulling forward to go faster. He would have run if she let go of him. The door to the stairs was so far away, and everyone seemed to be looking at the pair. She hoped they just appeared like a security agent escorting a patient somewhere, but her mind waited for the slightest hint of suspicion. The door came closer with each step, passing open doorways on the left and the right, people looking up and watching as they passed, TVs singing and talking as they did.

They reached the stairwell, and Vigil reached for the knob. It turned but the door didn't open. She tried again, jiggling the handle, praying she would feel it catch. Looking down the hall, a doctor and a nurse were having a discussion but kept glancing her way.

The nurse nodded her head at the doctor and turned towards the two, walking down the corridor towards them.

The doors were locked for security reasons – she should have figured as much – and Vigil pulled Westbrook's ID from her pocket, sliding it across the sensor pad. The door clicked and she turned the handle and opened it. Pushing Tyrone through first, Vigil looked back at the nurse as the door closed. The woman waved at her and quickened her pace.

The door clicked closed.

Turning to go down the stairs Tyrone stiffen beside her. A black man in a doctor's coat stood on the landing below.

With a roar Vigil launched herself through the air and down the stairs, fist pulled back to put the man out.

"No, wait!" the man yelled, failed to one knee and hunkering behind his upheld arms.

"Mom, don't!" Tyrone yelled at the same time.

Vigil landed, a foot on each side of the crouching man, her fist held up to strike. Looking from her target to her son, she asked, "Why?"

"He's Doctor Walters," Tyrone answered, "he's my doctor. He was nice to me."

"Not a good enough reason, Tyrone," she said, "He will try and stop us, and lock us both up."

"No," the doctor looked up from between his arms, "I won't. I promise. I came to help. When I saw you enter the room, I recognized you. I figured this would be your best escape route so I came here and waited."

"Why?" Vigil asked. "Why would you want to help us? You made us, and I am guessing you're making a lot of folks like us."

"No, it's not true," Walters lowered his hands, "we didn't make you. The T.A.L.O.N. Agency is refining some gene work blended with nanotechnology to create incredible results, but you're not one of our projects. And I want to help because not all of us believe what the Agency is doing is right. I believe in helping cure diseases, even improve the human condition, but not kidnapping and experimenting on unwilling or unknowing people."

"If you people didn't do this to me, how did it happen?" Vigil asked.

"All the tests implicate that you got it naturally, at least as far as we can tell. The most we know is that we didn't develop any strain that would trigger these latent and recessive genes. The Agency doesn't like that. Maybe nature is combatting our new ways, but your abilities were definitely turned on by a viral infection. Your son has those same genetic markers."

"Will he get the same abilities?"

"We don't know, but it is possible, even probable."

At the landing a half flight up, the door handle jiggled.

The doctor pulled a tablet from his coat pocket and keyed the screen.

Vigil's hand came back up, ready to smash either the device or the doctor.

The door buzzed, and locked with a click, the glass hazing over.

"I locked it," Walters said, his voice panicked when he realized she was ready again to hit him. "I will lock down the facility behind you. I can also set off alarms in a different part, so they think you're there. Don't hit me, please!"

"Ok," Vigil dropped her arm and waved Tyrone to her side. "But if you do anything to get us caught, you'd better hope and pray that you never see me again."

"I won't, now go. I will track you through Westbrook's ID and make sure no one gets too close to you."

"Fine, and, thank you."

"You're welcome; Tyrone's a good boy and deserves to be with people who love him." The doctor nodded at the boy, smiling.

The pair turned to go down the next set of stairs.

"Oh, wait!"

"What now?" Vigil asked, anger and exasperation in her voice.

"You're going to need to hit me, so it throws them off the thought that I helped you."

"They already think you might be," Tyrone said.

"Wha – How do you know?" Walters asked.

"I heard them talking, Specialist Westbrook and Agent Michaels, when you were asking me questions a couple days ago. They were behind the mirror, right?"

"Yeah, ok. Good to know. Well, too late now," the doctor looked up at Vigil and added, "You better make it look good then..."

He never had a chance to finish.

Her fist came down, snapping his head back. She grabbed him by his collar, tearing his coat and tie under the lab coat, and punched him in the ribs. They cracked. Then she slapped him and he stumbled back into the wall, the thud echoing as his head hit.

"Slight concussion, two broken ribs, and broken cardphone in your breast pocket where I tore your clothes. That should give them enough to think you didn't help, at least, not willingly. Thank you Doctor Walters, and good luck. We won't forget your help."

Without waiting for an answer Vigil took Tyrone by the shoulder again and turned down the stairs. Banging issued from the door above, and the doctor moaned, staggering to his feet. She hoped that he was still willing to help after what she did, but damn, it felt good. No one touched her son.

At the bottom of the stairs a door opened into a grassy area with benches. Opening it, Vigil looked around. Most people would be busy finishing up for the day and getting ready for shift change. They set off across the grass, her hand on her son's shoulder, heading for the car in the employee parking lot.

Behind them, distant alarms sounded from the building.

The green highway sign showed Regina was only five kilometers away. She had sent word to Tawana that things were fine and heading out of the country, insinuating that The Agency didn't have much control in South America.

But that was all behind them now. Ahead of them, Dawn waited for them with a spare room ready. Tyrone slept in the seat next to her and she smiled at him, touching his cheek. Hidden in the second largest city in Saskatchewan, they should be able to blend in well enough. And as soon as her son was settled in, Vigil would begin her patrol.

CASE 3718
CODENAME: SLEEPER CELL

"When I opened my eyes this time, after years of sleeping, I woke with the thought, 'I am the judge of the Earth,'" the creature explained to the small gathering. It was an eclectic handful of people disenchanted with their specie's social evolutionary path. A biologist, a journalist, a chemist, a psychologist, and an astrophysicist, all in the prime of their careers. "I shall decide if this planet lives and survives, or if it shall be stripped clean and left barren for whatever comes next. It won't be another primate species, though; I promise you that. You shall be the last chance for that line. If we can come to a peaceful agreement, and you can fulfill your mission to bring understanding to your selfish and violent species, then - and only then - can your species be allowed to survive."

The five women looked back and forth amongst one another, unsure how to react to these words, shifting in their makeshift seats of broken stalagmites. The Brazilian journalist made notes on her steno pad, her hand gliding across the page, sweat trickling down her long neck from her dark hair.

"Yes," the creature continued, running their hands down their sleek, pebbled-grey skin looking for any ruptures or lesions, "make notes. I have studied your species long enough to see the questions in your faces, etched into your foreheads. I can also see the fear and nervousness in your paled skin and dripping sweat. You can ask questions, I encourage it. It may be your questions that stop me from going back on this plan and beginning the destruction now."

"Why females?" the psychologist asked, raising her hand halfway before pulling it back down. She brought her chin up and spoke firmly, though her German accent was thicker than normal. "I mean, why are we all females? Is it because you think the females of our species are more easily cowed and bullied, or that we are more gullible or emotional?"

"No Doctor Blevins, it isn't any of those things," the creature's jaw creaked as they worked the long unused muscles. "Each time I have tried to reach out to humans, I have contacted males of your species. I did that because you are part of a patriarchal society and only recently have the females been given anything close to equality. This time I decided to speak to females because each and every time I have contacted males, they have gone mad. I think this is because they are too rigid in their thinking, and not able to conceive things beyond their own expectations. I am hoping females will be able to go beyond this."

"I am Cynthia Chen," the biologist stood as she spoke. "I am curious about you, of course. Historically there are myths and rumors of other beings visiting us, but you showed us the truth just before you disappeared almost three decades ago. Then we were contacted by Rayssa Oliveira and told you were ready to tell us the rest, and we were to come here."

The group looked at the Brazilian journalist, who looked up at the mention of her name.

Chen continued, "What exactly are you?"

The creature uncurled its two-meter long form and stretched. Sinew elongated, allowing it to reach the stalactites more than three meters above. "I am Zagreb, and I am a Troöd. My species came here more than three thousand years ago. I am neither male nor female; my species has the ability of sequential hermaphroditism. I tend to take on the form of a male among your kind since it is more likely to be treated with respect, but I have appeared as a female many times also."

Zagreb bent through their exercises, same as each time they woke after hibernation, designed to loosen and limber their body. "I don't know exactly how long I slept this time. In the past, it varied, perhaps a few years, perhaps a few centuries. It could be either – I have woken more and more frequently in the past hundred years – but I keep no time-tracking equipment. I can't risk it being detected while I sleep. And anything I build that may be seen, I make sure it fits in with the technology of the current culture. Before now I woke when the world spoke to me. Though I am only a visitor, my people have long been attuned to our environments, and I have been here long enough to become symbiotic with this one."

It was warm.

Sadness grew within the creature. The cave Zagreb slept in barely kept the warmth away. It must be fifteen or sixteen degrees Celsius; not nearly as chill as it should be this far underground. Zagreb had felt the warming trend for more than three and a half millennia. Each time they woke it was a little warmer.

The creatures that inhabited this world accelerated the situation, polluting and destroying natural filters in the ecosystem for almost as long as they had been building shelters.

"That answers little," Natalia Ivanova, the Russian Astrophysicist ran her hand through her short blonde hair, "where are you from? Why did you come here? Why are you judging our race and deciding its fate?"

The fifth woman, thin and mocha-skinned, spoke softly from her seat, her voice carrying the musical accent of her Ethiopian heritage, "I think Zagreb will get to all that. I am Adanech Adunga, and I work with biochemistry and astrochemistry, and have been a lead agent in particle accelerators for over ten years. I think Zagreb chose us because, as a group we will confront the facts and decide how to best bring the message to the world. We are all scientists of one sort or another, even the journalist studies human events and social habits. I think we should let this creature tell us what they want us know, and then ask questions to clarify the information they gave us. If I am not mistaken, Zagreb contacted each of us when we had just begun our college classes. Probably contacted many more than us too, but chose us for this meeting. I, for one, am fascinated and would like to hear what will be said."

The other women nodded and settled back onto their rocky perches, tablets, notepads, pens, and styluses at the ready.

Zagreb looked them over, shook their head as if to clear cobwebs, rubbed their large dark eyes, and nodded.

"Yes, I should explain. I trust each of you, as I knew you when you were younger by your race's standards. You were idealistic and hopeful and I hope your aging hasn't stolen those traits from you. I also hope you don't go mad, as the men did. I want to work with all of you, and don't want to kill any of you because your minds were too frail to handle the information." Zagreb shook their head again, squinting and rubbing their temples.

The women exchanged worried glances, a couple of them looking back towards the winding corridor that led to the outside world.

"I don't think that will be an issue though, as your minds are used to shifting and changing as needed, unlike men's. You also are used to making compromises, whereas the males of your species are prone to pushing until someone breaks and they get their own way. Let me tell you of my long stay on your planet, and we can come back to those concerns later.

"The last time I woke, I stayed among the people of this planet for well over a decade. I had woken deep under the Atlantic Ocean, where I had last fallen asleep after checking my deep trench machines that I had set up almost a century before. The machines are broken remnants of my people's technology, cobbled together from the scientific research equipment we had brought with us to study the oceans, skies, and lands of this planet more than three millennia earlier. I had shut them down in your calendar year of 1963, and knew I would be safe in the watery caves deep below the water's surface. They were monitoring your technological growth to see if your machines could do anything of use to me, sometimes drawing machines into their watery grasp so they could be evaluated for use. This caused worry and strife among your kind, and it had to be brought to an end as your technology expanded and I risked detection.

"When I woke, my machines told your technology had grown, but not so much as to be able to allow me to contact my people or travel home. I knew the repetitive comet that you call Halley's would make its rounds soon. I had spoken to a man, a writer, almost a century earlier about it. That man witnessed the first photographs of this celestial body. The humans had grown in technology, but were still primitive then, even in the decade they termed the 1980s." Zagreb took the form of a man, smoothing their pebbled skin and rounding their features. Their jaw fattened, and their shoulders broadened. "When I came from the Atlantic Ocean, I took a swimmer in the deep waters off the coast of Bermuda for his swimming gear. Once on land, I changed again for more appropriate land clothing and currency of the people."

"What do you mean, 'took a swimmer' and 'changed again'?" Chen asked. "Did you mimic someone, or become a composite of your own creation?"

"I found a suitable person to mimic, then I removed them so it would not cause confusion or a problem for me."

"You murdered someone and took on their face?" Oliveira's bronze skin paled.

"Yes, in these cases I did," Zagreb's voice was steady, "it was necessary so I could blend in with a social group. I scanned the brain patterns of each person and gained familiarity with their family and social group, allowing me much quicker access to the things I needed. My species can communicate in a limited fashion telepathically. It is a simple matter of energy resonance. Your primitive brains are just beginning to reach this stage, and usually by some genetic abnormality."

Zagreb looked across the five women's faces and saw the fear; though they could also see concern that they may be reading their thoughts. Zagreb didn't need to, they could clearly see the fight or flight reaction triggered by their innate morality and sense of hurt at someone of their species being killed at the hands of someone not of their species.

Humans fascinated Zagreb. They could watch hours of reports of murders, rapes, and worse and not think a thing about it, but let someone from a different social or economic group attack one of their own and they would tear down a city in their rage.

"Allow me to assure you, this is not always the way," Zagreb said, their now - human and too - pink face smiling at them as Zagreb stood naked before them, "I am able to make a composite of any type of your species I would like, but in this case it was merely more expeditious for me to do it that way. I don't understand the need for clothing as fashion or individuality. Or money as a matter of trade. My body adjusts to the environment so the former isn't needed, unlike yours, and my society had no use for the latter. But I knew that to blend in with these people, I would need more than to just appear of the same flesh. After all, I have been doing this since before the Egyptian dynasties."

He looked at them again, and then did a very human sigh. "You may rest easy, you are in no danger from me. Though I may appear as a female or male of your race, I have no need to mimic anyone this time.

"To continue, I made my way to the Florida coast, seeking the Naval Base and Port of Canaveral, though I later learned it had been changed to Cape Kennedy the same year I went to sleep. It did cause some raised eyebrows when I asked for it by a name that hadn't been used for twenty years. I did know that the people of this world were expanding from destructive missiles to craft that would leave this planet's atmosphere, and that is where they were doing it.

"When I investigated, I found that your space program had advanced significantly since I was last awake two decades before. They were planning to launch a handful of probes to study the comet, the same comet that had come in 1910 and returning every three quarters of a century since time immemorial. Unknown to the public, they were also launching a manned shuttle to observe it. The machines were still primitive, but the men were creative and the only real threat to my plans. In just under a year, I had infiltrated the government by changing my appearance again, and sabotaged the manned flight. As I mentioned before, your people are capable of amazing empathy, and it showed when the shuttle exploded shortly after its launch. I needed to know more, and I had hoped you had changed and evolved away from war and violence.

"After that had been handled, I changed form again, and took on the identity of Betty, a spiritual healer and writer. As Betty, I wrote about the spirit world – the closest I could get to explaining how my people traveled without revealing too much and causing suspicion by your government and scientific community. I was contacted by a man named David, and befriended by him. I revealed certain information to David, hoping he would be key in bringing an open conversation between myself and your people. I told the man that he would write five books in three years, and ideas and information would pass through him, though he may sometimes not understand the meaning, to enlighten the world. I opened that human to the energies I can feel, hoping to create an ambassador of sorts. It was a simple matter of altering the brain chemistry of the man. I also told David that within twenty years a machine would be invented that would allow travel in ways that time would have no meaning, which would have been the truth if things had gone differently. I wasn't totally wrong, the Large Hadron Collider was built, but much of its abilities have been hidden, largely by an organization called The T.A.L.O.N. Agency. I also warned the human about the destabilization of the seabed because of oil drilling. I was very worried about my deep sea equipment being discovered or destroyed through human carelessness about the environment as they sought your crude energy source.

"The man, David, went mad in a way, thinking he was in contact with the source of creation and receiving information that made him a prophet of sorts. This was the same era when your people were creating the myth of alien visitors. Beings of grey and green skin that fly in saucers through the sky. Yes, my species has those color skins, and the drawings and movies do resemble what is now my native form, but they had it all wrong. So did David. He spoke of a race of lizard beings that could change shape and control human society from the shadows. The man claimed the leaders of the most powerful free countries were these alien beings. He completely misinterpreted my message, and I had to abandon the man before he did more harm, and left him to his own devices. Some listened to David, but most thought him to be crazy, and the governments did everything they could to help this idea of insanity. The man had good intentions, wanting to stop disease and destruction, but couldn't be trusted further.

"Before sleeping again, in the beginning of the new millennium, I traveled to a research station in the deep southern Pacific Ocean trenches to check my equipment. This is where I came after that, in the caves of the Andes Mountains in South America. The machines I had collected in the Atlantic Ocean allowed me to repair the scientific research station in the Pacific and activate it, to potentially devastating results. It created a "Bloop", a sound that was heard for thousands of kilometers around. Your people panicked. Some joked that the writer, Lovecraft, whom I had befriended in 1910, had wrote of a creature in the deep that had now been awoken. He only wrote about that because I mentioned my work station to him, as well as explained genetic manipulation and some of the creatures I had grown during my stay here. But I will tell you more about that later. They didn't know how close to being right they were. I had finished calibrating the machines to contact my people, so it would be ready on the next pass of the comet in 2061 and use it as a broadcasting antenna, then shut it down before it could be located. The governments assured people that it was simply the sound of an iceberg scraping the ocean floor, but they didn't believe it themselves. I had to carefully conceal my equipment and lay out false trails so it wouldn't be found. I even created false underwater bunkers to draw attention away from my machines. It is that equipment that I need to check on now. It is less than three decades until the comet returned, and the next step in my plan needed to be put into action."

Zagreb stared at the woman in the opening of the cave; Oliveira gasped for breath. The creature had met her shortly before going to sleep again, hidden in the caves of the southern continent of the Americas, deep in the rain forest. Now the girl Zagreb had known had grown into a woman, and aged into her middle years. Rayssa was a thin woman and he guessed she would be considered handsome to her own kind.

"How did you know where to find me?" Zagreb hissed, their non-human tongue slipping into a sibilant whisper.

The other women stared at Oliveira.

"You set up genetic markers, didn't you? Created hybrids of creatures with humans." She looked at the alien over her shoulder, her hand on the wall holding her up. "I heard a report of a huge reptilian humanoid creature emerging from the sea in Atlantic City that was taken down, and of a half snake, half human also. Was that you?"

"Yes, that was me. It was one of my genetic mutations, and it was triggered by pollution levels in the ocean. If humans didn't keep destroying their environment, the creature would have never been able to mature and would have died without notice. As I said, it is not the first time I did this. Humans are like an infestation, which insist on living outside of nature, rather than with it. They create plastic vehicles, making a foreign substance that the planet cannot reabsorb. They mine the metal veins in the planet, destroying the very foundation of the land they walk upon. You need to change, or you will destroy yourselves."

"Isn't that our right though?" the reporter spat, turning to face Zagreb.

The other women sat motionless, worried that the Brazilian's temper would trigger the same in the creature.

"Yes, but no," Zagreb said, their tone patient. "If you merely destroyed yourself, it would be acceptable, but you destroy everything around you, killing hundreds and thousands of other species of plants and animals, crippling the whole ecosystem. Is that fair? Is it right that you decide the fate of every species on this world? No, I do not think it is. They live within nature and deserve life, and the ability to go forward. They don't deserve to be killed by your poisons, and choke on your plastic roads, or your careless energy usage."

"You don't know what it is like to be human, to fight against these things. We don't all want that."

"Then fight against it, instead of waiting to be spoon fed what to think through your entertainment shows. Climate change wakes me. It has happened before, I am a Troöd. I have become more human, and less Troöd throughout the centuries, trying to understand your species better. I can only hope that new human technology allows me to contact my people, to warn them away or perhaps bring them back to Earth to destroy humans so the rest of the world may survive. I will connect to Halley's Comet as an antenna in 2062. I need this time to prepare, and I hope that you five are the beginning of the redemption of your people. Even if I am successful, my people won't be able to even return a message until 2138 when the comet returns past Earth, and then won't arrive until after the next time the comet comes around. Please, hear me out. Surely you five can kill me easily if you think I am a threat? What can it hurt to have the greatest mysteries of your planet's history explained and revealed before you have to decide that?"

Oliveira nodded, and returned to her seat, almost falling into it and the Russian Astrophysicist, Ivanova, steadied her.

"I recall waking in the Pacific Ocean," Zagreb continued, the women looking back to them, "I didn't know it then, but it was 8:15 a.m. on August 6, 1945. The Earth screamed. It was electromagnetic waves, disturbed by an explosion on the island of Japan, but it was more than that. The electromagnetic waves of human thought were screaming too. Humans put out an energy frequency, and the frequency was alive with terror and aggression. A bomb had been dropped that ended life. Nothing would be the same after that. A weapon of massive destructive power had crashed through the human collective psyche, tearing a hole in the innocence of mankind. It was the bombing of Hiroshima.

"I explored the planet again, for the next half dozen years. These weapons were being tested everywhere. In the oceans, killing countless fish and mammals in the waters. On land, destroying areas and the surrounding ecosystem. It amazed me, once again, the capacity your kind has for destruction. No wonder man had been considered a plague of vermin. Destroying in their wake, claiming they were conquering their world. You don't conquer a planet. If you try and do that, it will tun out bad. The planet will win. It will always win.

"You live outside of nature, not with it. You are an infestation that eats away at the very structure you need to survive. You are guaranteeing your own destruction.

"My people have learned to alter their own genetic structure, and the genes of other species, to create new things. This has been used to further our race,- as well as create soldiers, scientists, and more that are adaptable to environments we could not normally survive in. I used this science to create huge cephalopods, not very unlike my own species when we first arrived on this planet, though we were not much larger than men. In 1730, I grew a squid-like creature, altering it in size and temperament, to combat the growing problem of whaling. It was labeled the kraken by your species, and it was seen in many oceans. It was bred to attack the ships that threatened its food source, whales. It didn't last long, as breeding became an issue. The huge creatures each sought their own hunting grounds, so they rarely crossed paths to reproduce. When they did meet, they often fought over the territory.

"In 1871 I created a creature that combined my own amphibious genes with an aquatic dinosaur. I designed it to be fresh or salt water, and many made their ways across land to different lakes. Your people saw some of them on occasion, spreading panic and wonder when they did. The issue of breeding again was an issue, because they were so far separated from one another. The most famous ended up in Loch Ness on the island known as Scotland. I don't recall why I made these. I think I was just lonely and they reminded me of home.

"Ten years later, I activated the machine of our science station in the Atlantic Ocean. This was meant to attract and collect ships and other technology from you. I meant to study you and find a way to contact my people using your technology, since my own had been destroyed. If I could I would bring more of my people here, to help find our missing scientists and perhaps once again contact your people.

"The machine ran for four score years before I decided that your people had reached a point where they would detect my activities. I couldn't risk being found, or my technology. But before going to rest again, I ventured onto land, onto the continent of the Northern Americas. I met a brilliant and reclusive young writer named Howard. I thought I could befriend him and give him information about myself and my people. I don't know why I tried this again; each time I have it has failed miserably. Confiding in him, I told him my history, and the history of the scientific excursion that brought me here. I told him the philosophy of my people, what he took as a religion. This knowledge was too much for him, and drove him mad. He later would create stories in his madness, including myths about planet eating monstrosities and others that lay dormant under the ocean waves, waiting to wake and devour your people. You have such delicate minds, largely due to the fact that your brains are still developing. Perhaps there will be more promise of working with the chimpanzees in the continent of Africa or the Capuchin Monkeys of the country of Brazil - that have entered their own stone age - once they develop.

"The information I give seems to have an effect of paranoia and fear upon humans. Like your brains just can't grasp what would be simple concepts to any Troöd still in school. You all seem to lean towards believing everything is against you, or that you as an individual are so special you are the voice of a god.

"Before parting ways with Lovecraft, I learned about Halley's Comet. The year I spent with the man was the first time the comet was photographed. I realized then that I could harness that comet and use it as a communication device, sending a message to my people from the deep reaches of space, but I needed to plant a device on the comet itself. Your technology was not to that point though. It is barely there now.

"I share with you now, as I did with him then. And I fear for your sanity also. Every person I have shared this with has fallen to delusions and falling away from sanity. I hope you will be different.

"I recall one time I awoke just after the turn of the century, around 1400. Your people were just coming out of their haze of the Dark Ages. The Western world was feeling the birth pangs of science, and the world stood aghast as age-old beliefs were targeted, threatened, and shattered. I wanted to help. It could have been a turning point for humanity, the gaining of awareness larger than of their own small importance and large egos.

"I wrote a book, in the script of my people. I thought about doing it in a human language, but there were so many and no one could create a unifying language. And that is the secret to bringing the world together: one language. If everyone is able to communicate, it takes away so much fear shrouded in mystery and brings understanding. But man has never been able to do that have they?

"The book I wrote cataloged botanical notes, including hand drawn pictures since photography was nearly half a millennia in the future. I also charted the stars, planets, comets, and the moons visible to this planet. I detailed the biology of your kind's reproductive systems, and ways you could better your own biology through biochemistry and genetic alteration during the natal periods. This is when you are most susceptible to those sorts of things. This included medicines from various plants that would fix simple ailments such as cancer and more.

"When I went into hibernation afterwards, I gave it to a wealthy family that actively supported the arts and sciences. The book disappeared after I did. It reemerged a little over a hundred years ago, from what I understand. At the start of your first great world war, a man named Voynich bought it from a Jesuit College near Rome. It has since ended up in the Beinecke Library, though you can purchase electronic copies for a pittance. No one has ever translated it, or uncovered the secrets I tried to share. I wanted to help, but it went nowhere. Man will not listen. They never have, not since my people first came to this planet.

"I remember once, I saved a whole region from drought, showing them ways of irrigation. I acted as an advisor to powerful men, bringing a new age to that area. In 1094 they named a city in Croatia named after me. A city named Zagreb. I don't know if it still stands, but I think of it once in a while.

"I wasn't always so altruistic. A hundred years before I wrote that book, around 1300, I introduced a dark plague that neatly wiped out a significant portion of your population. I thought to make man start over, and perhaps then you would seek other means than violence and aggression as a solution. Around 400 I engineered the undermining of Rome, steering them to the destructive insanity that comes with greed and gluttony.

"Just before your first century ended, I was mad with vengeance, sorely missing my people and still mourning the death of the thousands of peaceful scientists that came to this planet with me. I set out to create a reaction in a volcano to destroy the angry creatures that destroyed my people and our research station. That was nearly 700 years after I spoke to the first human I chose to confide in about my people. Plato got it all wrong, but he also wrapped it in a story, shifting the events I told him about by thousands of years so people wouldn't think he was insane by claiming the things he wrote was true.

"I had dealings with your people before that, well since our first contact. It was more than seven hundred years before the fall of Rome, when I was in Greece and revealed my people's plans to a human for the first time since your people destroyed our research station thirteen centuries earlier. His name was Plato, and though he took down the history well enough, he changed things about the story. He made us human and told everyone that it happened nine thousand years previous. He was smart enough to not want to either be ridiculed by his community, or perhaps he saw the danger of revealing the truth. I don't think he went mad. He tried to give humankind a lesson.

"There were other times I tried to help your kind. I once opened a trade route between the Egyptian Empire and the people of the Southern American continent. It took less than a decade before they fell to trading mood altering plants. Tobacco and coca leaves traveled the ocean more than people. Tobacco created a much stronger effect on your kind back then. You've built an amazing tolerance to it over the last couple centuries. Even when the Europeans were colonizing the Northern American continent, they would only need a thimble-sized pipe to smoke of tobacco. Now, I see cigars and shake my head in dismay at what you've done to your bodies.

"On behalf of my people, I have studied yours for more than four millennia. I have watched your growth and ingenuity conflict with your primitive aggressions and proclivity to try and control everything around you. Those last two things make you destructive, and you fight to tame anything you see, even each other. Doing this with your world will not allow you to survive. You will destroy your world's ecosystem, and in turn, kill yourselves. And the most distressing part is that you will blame someone else."

"Are there others of your kind?" Chen leaned forward on her perch.

"I don't know," Zagreb wiped their brow in a very human gesture, "I think so, I think I see traces or what could be signs from them. But none have ever found my machines. Perhaps they were hunted and killed, or went mad. Perhaps David was right and some have taken positions of high power in your government. Perhaps the rumors of the green and grey aliens are not just myth, but others of my species trying to build life boats to abandon this accursed planet of yours. There may have been a few amongst your early cultures. I look at the Egyptian, Norse, Central American and other gods and wonder if that were my fellows trying to make a better world by giving your kind guidance.

"When we landed here, the closest beings on the planet that we resembled was the octopus. They could have been a distant and primitive ancestor of ours, an alternate branch of evolution, similar to your great apes to you. We were primarily aquatic, though we had a dual nature and were amphibious, so we could study the landmasses. When we encountered intelligent life, which we hadn't realized was here because you did not inhabit the oceans, we were thrilled. We had long sought allies across the stars and dimensions. Upon first contact, your kind feared us or worshiped us, but mostly the former. They staged attacks and sought to chase us away. We understood our bodies were alien in nature, so we modified ourselves, changing our genetic coding and becoming more like you. Some of us even blended into your societies, as I do today, to learn more about you.

"We were eventually accepted, or so we thought. Your people came to us to learn and study and we welcomed you. And in 1630 BCE, we were betrayed. As our research station floated outside in the Atlantic Ocean, just outside the straits of Gibraltar and to the west of the Mediterranean Sea, hundreds of ships attacked us. Ships of all nations came together to surge over our, well, Plato called it an island, even a continent, and described it well enough. The raiders made their way into the interior of our station and destroyed the delicate equipment. Wonders your kind are just beginning to imagine were at our finger tips before your people began building huts to live in.

"Your people, in their ignorance, triggered equipment we had inside a volcano at Santorinas, destroying our vessel, and ironically, Crete and the Minoan Empire who led the attack against us. This volcano was like no other your people had encountered. The sound of the explosion was heard on the Eastern Coast of the Northern American Continent, the southern tip of the African continent, and deep into the interior of the Asian continent. It created a giant wave that rolled across Greece, Crete, and many other places going almost two kilometers inland. The soot darkened the sky for almost a week and rained upon the land for many more weeks. The Minoans sunk their own fleet, and crippled our exploration outpost in the act. I guess they succeeded. And in legend, Plato named us Atlantis."

The soft thumps of air darts hissed through the small cavern. The satchel on the floor in front of the Troöd exploded with the most gentle of sounds, pieces of leather and linen floated in the air and drifted to the ground. Four of the women slumped to the ground, only the German psychologist remained conscious, and she stared at Zagreb through slitted eyes.

"So, you shall be my betrayer," the Troöd plucked a half-dozen centimeter-long needles from their hide.

"You altered your skin, thickening it?" Doctor Blevins raised herself from behind the boulder where she had crouched, hands held in front of her in a martial arts stance. "You expected an attack?"

"Genevie, I always expect an attack when I deal with humans. Don't worry, I am not going to harm you."

"Oh, I am confident of that," the Doctor snatched a sticky grenade from inside her jacket and tossed it at the creature.

Zagreb slid from their human form, taking on their more natural appearance and slithered up a wall. The device detonated, spraying thin viscous threads towards them. The creature was caught in part of the blast, and the silk-like filaments coated half of their body, adhering them to the wall.

"Good, don't go anywhere," Doctor Blevins hooked her hands

under the arms of the Asian biologist and dragged her towards the exit, "I will be right back, I need to go call for our ride."

The two women disappeared around the corner and Zagreb sighed, one of the many human mannerisms that clung to them even in their natural form. They tested the strength of the web, seeing if they could pull free. Their skin stretched then began to tear. They settled in and began a more subtle change of their biochemistry.

"Still hanging around, I see." Doctor Blevins returned for the next woman.

"Why are you taking them? You don't need them, not when you have me."

"The T.A.L.O.N. Agency wants them, as much to collaborate my story as to use their specific skill sets in studying you and finding your hidden machines and how to use that technology. The journalist will set a spin to your story and print what we need her to, so The Agency comes out ahead," she patted the Brazilian woman's unconscious form before linking her arms under the woman's arms, "and her research skills will help find the locations you hid things. The biologist and chemist will be handy in studying you, after all you did mention doing genetic modification to yourself. That would be a handy trick rather than waiting for the next generation to grow with the seeded alterations. And the astrophysicist along with the chemist will be handy in dealing with calculations to find your homeworld and realigning the LHC to help track it."

Her voice trailed off as she disappeared with the second woman down the corridor.

Zagreb tested the filaments again, closed their eyes, and made adjustments to their biochemistry.

Blevins returned and began dragging the Ethiopian chemist away.

"Why couldn't I feel your surface thoughts?" Zagreb asked, their eyes still closed. "I should have been able to detect the betrayal."

"Silly lizard, I have two hair combs that create a neural net of sorts, blocking any bioelectromagnetic pulses escaping or entering my head." The woman's voice was staggered by puffs of breath from her exertion and grew dimmer as she dragged the other woman away. "At least anything small, a burst from the right source would easily break through that defense, but we had to be subtle."

When Blevins returned for the astrophysicist, Ivanova, Zagreb had turned around in the web and now faced her, the creature's skin slick with perspiration. Zagreb watched through glossy black eyes that were all pupil.

"I hoped," the Troöd began, "I still hope, that you humans could be friends and allies. Reconsider this Genevie, leave the agency and help me bring in a new age that can help your species grow as you never have before."

"Begging now?" Blevins gathered the final woman's limp form, preparing to drag it out with the others. "When I was younger, I thought a lot about what you told me when we first met. When I met the Agency, I saw more than you ever told me. I saw the reports of the dimensional wormholes that brought raptors to Oklahoma City more than three decades ago. I saw a mere glimpse of what man would become and what he could do, and I knew I had to tell someone about you. They explained it to me, showed me your greater plan to bring your people back here and control us, experiment on us, and enslave us through fear so we worshiped you."

"That is not the way of my people," Zagreb interrupted.

"You may say that," Blevins said, dragging the last woman down the tunnel, "but what you told us here today says something very different."

Zagreb slipped from the threads, the coating on their flesh neutralizing the bonding agent in the web. The Troöd walked in a circle around the small sanctuary. The creature would be leaving in a few moments. As Zagreb heard the psychologists footsteps approach they blended into the wall and watched her.

She looked around, shining a flashlight at the spot where they had been restrained, her eyes widening when she didn't find them.

"You spoke to them before today, didn't you? Assessed them, and helped bring fear of me into their minds. I saw it on their thoughts. You turned them against me before I even woke."

Hoverchoppers hummed and thumped, floating above the trees outside, the sound echoing through the cavern.

Blevins looked around, her eyes wide with panic.

"You won't get away!" She yelled, backing away and pulling a small device from her jacket pocket. "I will seal you in. It would be better to have you dead than not have you at all!"

The woman turned and ran, a series of sparks showering the hall outside the hollow Zagreb stood in. Explosions sounded and rocks cracked and fell. Zagreb slid into a fissure in the wall, and pulled himself up by touch using the handholds he had carved decades before. He slid his body into a lava tube barely as wide as a man's thigh and slithered upward, following it to where it would lead him to freedom. The Troöd knew what he had to do, he had known it all along, but had hoped that this time would be different.

CASE 4943
CODENAME: BAD LUCK JIMMY

Jimmy crumpled to his knees, gasping for breath. Ears ringing, he tried to suck in air. The sound of his mother shouting echoed off the alley walls, dulled by the sound of the wireless earbuds pumping music into his ears. He looked up; with her purse, she was pummeling one of three teens who cornered them after leaving the movieplex downtown.

"Leave my son alone, you hooligan!" his mom yelled, swinging her handbag wildly and missing.

The kid laughed at her and put his hand over her face and shoved her to the ground. The woman fell with a heavy thud and her head rang against the dumpster as it connected, her pocketbook flying to the center of the alley.

"Need your mommy to protect you, Jimmy? You pathetic creeper. Can she handle a real man?" the young tough walked over to her and kicked her in the ribs. She slid another foot with the blow, but didn't move otherwise. Another of the boys picked up her purse and rummaged through it.

"Still working at the coffee café? Creeping out all the little girls who come in? Well, lemme show you what we think of that?" said the third guy, approaching Jimmy, a sneer on his face.

"Hey man," the first boy shouted to his friends, "she ain't moving. I think she's hurt. We may have even killed her! We need to get out of here!"

"Don't you tell anyone about us, you got it, loser?" the third kid said, and kicked Jimmy in the head.

The world went black.

"Bad Luck Jimmy," Officer Williams poked at the screen of his police cardphone, "looks like you got lucky this time, unlike your mom."

"I got lucky with his mom once, worse three bucks I ever spent," Officer Vanzetti looked at the blanket-wrapped, hunched form of Jimmy.

"And that was for the cream for the rash afterwards, I bet." Both men laughed and high fived each other.

"Hey," the female EMT attending Jimmy said from where they sat inside the ambulance, "leave him alone. He just had a traumatic experience."

"His whole life has been a traumatic experience," the first cop muttered, turning away. "I should know, I went to school with this loser."

"Don't listen to them, sir," the woman said, "I believe you're a fine man, and I'm sorry for what happened here today. All of it. I am sure you're not anything they say."

"No," Jimmy choked back tears and pushed his second earbud back into his ear. A classic song from decades before, Bonnie Tyler singing Holding Out for a Hero, played for him. He slumped further and his greasy black hair fell over his eyes as music thrummed a superhero theme song. "They're right. I always get the crap end of the stick. I'm a complete loser."

"James Earnest Weinbaum, there's a reason you have always been known as Bad Luck Jimmy, and that's because people always said you were the biggest loser ever. Not that I ever said that, you know I'm your best friend and I know how awesome you are," Wendell said, leaning back and popping a cheese puff into his mouth. "Just ask anyone who had ever known you. You were the zit-faced kid when we was in school, picked on 'cause you was short, wore hand-me-downs from second-hand stores, and preferred to read or play

Dungeons and Dragons instead of sports. I mean, usually with me, but I wasn't Mr. Popularity, either. You knew all the lines from The Force Awakens and most of the super hero movies that came out when you was a kid. Remember that one time you brought your cape to school when you was in seventh grade, and teacher had to pull three bigger kids off of you – I would have helped you out, but I already had a wedgie and was shoved into the trash can – the kids who had gone from calling you names, to shoving you, to punching and kicking you. Sure, the staff seemed sympathetic but we heard them later saying things like 'he's asking to be beat up, wearing a cape to school' or 'when's that kid going learn that being a spaz won't make you any friends'. Dude, you suck."

Wendell stared at his best friend and continued to pop cheese puffs into his mouth, washing it down with a triple caffeinated lime green craft soda from the local shop, Craft Brews by Blues. Wendell went back to poking his cardphone and switching through the channels on the laser screen of the TV. Jimmy slouched in a worn recliner watching his friend. Wendell could hear the strains of some soundtrack coming from Jimmy's earbuds.

"You know Wendell," Jimmy stood up, his voice nasal and high pitched, "you're rough, but honest. You ain't no prize yourself. Maybe put down the snack bag you strap on, and drink some water, or at least diet something."

"I'm fine like I am. More of me to love, you know how the ladies love the double dad bod, bud!"

"So, are you going to do this with me?" Jimmy stepped forward, bumping into the table and knocking over a drink. He ran to the kitchen for a towel, tripping over the edge of the carpet as he returned.

"Do what? Train and become a super hero? That is crazy talk man. You trip over your own shoe laces more than anyone I have ever met. If you meet a woman, you're as likely to spill your drink on her as shake her hand. Man, you cross the street to get out of the way of high-school kids, and you think you're going to face down some criminals? How many gimmie vids you been sucking up? Or is it too many microwave meals, and the radiation got to your brain? Bro, just relax. Your mom just died, you got a bit of money, you bought a new laser screen, and you think you're going to sell everything in the house and become Batman or Iron-Man?"

"Yeah, but no." Jimmy wiped at the table, dribbling the soda onto the remote. He picked it up and wiped it across the superhero logo on his t-shirt. "I think I got something more going on. I still need to work out, get fit…"

"Duder, something else going on? Like what? You got some psychic powers going on? The meteorites infect you with alien DNA and make you bullet proof? What you got going on that I ain't seen?"

"Wendell, this is the plan; I am selling all the furniture and turning this room into my HQ. Getting a new computer that can handle all the G-Flow I need, taking in information as it hits the police scanners and Twitter. It will distill it into what I need to know, and then feed it to me via gear." Jimmy held up a finger to stop Wendell from interrupting again. "But that's not all, no sir, my dear rotund sidekick, I will train you to use the equipment here, while I hit the streets. Ah, ah, ah, don't interrupt yet. I have more.

"The garage will be my workout room, I already have things coming. I will take one year to learn yoga and tai chi to prepare my mind and body. I will spend one more year learning different fighting forms: taekwondo, boxing, kendo, whatever I can. I will practice these skills every day for at least five hours a day. I will spend five more honing my mind, learning new languages, computer skills, and things like that. And I will spend five hours learning the city, from top to bottom. Making contacts, and so on. So, what do you think?"

"I think you're crazy, but you got a good TV. I'll stick around and at least get a good laugh from this."

Breathe, Jimmy thought, matching his jogging rhythm to the music in his ears. Queen's song *Flash* pushed him on. *He'll save every one of us. Jimmy wanted to be that hero.*

He felt better, his body coming along well enough. In three months, he had lost thirty pounds and added muscle. The slow techniques of the yoga and tai chi, along with the breathing exercises, had given him coordination he never knew he could possess. He could watch TV shows in Spanish and French and understand most of what was said, but the app on his cardphone helped. He would begin learning Russian and Farsi soon.

Breathe.

In three months, he had turned his mother's house into a good base of operations. It wasn't reasonable to use the living room as he had originally planned, so his basement bedroom had been set up as the computer center. The garage was needed for the equipment he had ordered, so his living room became a workout room. His favorite change was a sound system through the whole house with his custom playlist constantly playing.

Breathe.

His digi-contacts that fixed his vision also transmitted the view of his suburban neighborhood back to the house. Electronic glasses that adjusted to light intensity with a wraparound display replaced his earbuds, feeding the music directly into a microchips placed against his skull, behind his ears. The police band could be heard through the music, and he was learning the codes and lingo pretty well. Wendell crunched chips in his ear, making commentary on the movie on one of the four screens, and the video feed on another.

Breathe, Jimmy thought, turning into the local playground to use the chin-up bars. He punched a different playlist on the cardphone strapped to his wrist to better suit this exercise. Pushups on the teeter totter would follow. He no longer even noticed the weights on his ankles and wrists. That would complete his outdoor workout, and then he could return home for weightlifting and practicing with the bag.

Kids and parents didn't pay him much mind, not like they did the first few weeks, when he would show up out of breath and red in the face. They used to laugh as he tried and failed to jump up to the chin-up bar, or when he tripped over his own feet just walking. Kids would shout insults about his greasy hair, and he would look away. With the exercise, he had begun showering twice a day now, and though his hair was long, it was no longer greasy. Some of the mothers even eyed him with appreciation. At least, he thought it looked like that.

No time for that, he thought, I lost my own mother, and now I have to stop anyone else from losing theirs.

"Bad Luck Jimmy," Officer Williams watched the once-slouched man exit the dojo, "well, I'll be damned. Check this out, Vanzetti."

Both officers watched the man walk down the street. It had been six months since they had seen him in the back of the ambulance. Jimmy's shoulders were back and he looked around as he walked, as if he were watching for something. He stepped with care, every movement with purpose. He moved with grace that hadn't been there before.

"Wanna mess with him?" Vanzetti asked.

"Oh hell yeah!" Williams answered, and both men stepped away from the wall in front of the coffee cafe where they leaned. They swaggered forward, one hand on their weapon, the other carrying a coffee cup.

"Hey Bad Luck Jimmy, you get a haircut?" Williams called.

Jimmy stopped, his head turning a moment before his body, and faced them.

"Yes officers?" Jimmy didn't rush his words. He looked both men up and down, his eyes stopping for just a second on the men's hands.

"Oh, you been working out? Thinking you're all tough now?" Williams taunted.

"Aw dude," Wendell said in his ear, "Play it cool."

"Yes, officer. And no." Jimmy kept his voice even, matching the beat of the music in his ears.

"Buddy, that was funny, but it wasn't cool," around a mouthful of food.

"What the hell does that mean, loser? You messing with us?" Williams stepped forward, his shoulders shooting backwards and his chest puffing out.

"No, sir. It means I have been working out, but I don't think I am all tough. Yet."

"You had to add 'yet'? You trying to incite police violence?" Wendell sounded worried.

"Yet?" Williams laughed. "Yet? You getting all pumped up so you don't get picked on anymore? I bet you trip and fall on your face when you turn and leave. Which you better do right now, understand? Get to stepping."

Jimmy's eyes narrowed and his forehead wrinkled for moment before he turned, his movements measured and even, and walked away.

"You got a problem?" Williams barked at Jimmy.

"Just keep walking, don't turn back." Wendell advised.

Jimmy stopped again and turned back, once again his head turning and his body following, his eyes scanning around him. "No, sir. But you may. Do you?"

"Bro, what the hell?" Wendell sputtered into Jimmy's ear. "Did you lose your common sense with all that weight?"

"What did you say to me?" Williams took a step towards Jimmy.

The sound of brakes squealing and a horn ripped through the air. Williams stumbled over a crack in the sidewalk, his coffee hit his chest and the top flew off. Hot coffee spilled down his front and he screamed and leapt backwards, tripping over the same crack. The coffee doused him as he landed on his butt on the sidewalk.

Jimmy turned and walked away as Officer Williams sat swearing and Vanzetti tried to help him to his feet, only succeeding in spilling his own coffee over his flailing partner.

"Oh jeebs!" Wendell cried. "That was awesome, and I got it all on video from the glasses!"

Jimmy walked down the street, his hands in his pockets, but his chin up. The sounds of traffic hummed under the music in his ears. Spanish voices could also be heard from the people on the sidewalk passing him. Most looked down, and didn't make eye contact. The few that did almost always looked away once he glanced in their direction. The rare person that continued to stare at him received a casual glance in return before he looked elsewhere. But he noted which ones did that.

The body armor didn't show under the light jacket Jimmy wore. He didn't notice the weight after nine months of working out every day. His leather gloves hid the metal plates on his knuckles and the back of his hand. The battery pack on his belt could turn those into a contact Taser with a twitch of his wrist, or launch metal probes on wires as far as thirty feet. The flashlight in his belt holster concealed an extendable baton in its handle, and a knife was strapped to each of his calves under his pants.

Nine months of training had brought a level of calm confidence to Jimmy, and he was no longer anxious when walking the streets of the city. His mother would be proud of him.

He scanned the area ahead of him, the heads up readout of his glasses recording license plates and cross-referencing faces with public data bases. Social media found almost everyone now, showing him names and other information. Public records pulled up misdemeanors and felonies on every twentieth person. Most were not worth paying attention to, but Wendell stored each and every bit of information that came across three out of four computer screens back home. The fourth was for day trading, which Wendell played like a video game, and invested Jimmy's remaining money from minute to minute. When not tracking the market, it still played some movie to keep Wendell from getting bored between snacks, but even his friend was more interested in what was going on than a movie most days.

"Hey Jimmy," Officer Vanzetti nodded, he and Williams passing Jimmy as they walked their beat.

Jimmy nodded to them, data appearing on his display about the two officers, showing commendations, arrest records, and any disciplinary actions that had been made public. Links to newspaper articles or social media also came up. Two days ago Jimmy had passed T.A.L.O.N. Agency agents, but almost no information showed about them.

"Why did you even speak to him?" Williams growled.

"He's ok, just forget about him," Vanzetti answered as they passed out of hearing range.

Jimmy had lived in this city his whole life, but it was like a new place. The noise of the street was different than it had been when he was a kid. The electric cars had replaced the gas and oil models of his childhood. The hum of tires blended with the hum of rechargeable engines, and the smell was different. A slight smell of ozone, but no more exhaust like it was in the old days. No one played loud music like they had, besides the occasional car. But people didn't have vehicles liked they used to, either. Most folks relied on the buses, trains, and other public transportation. You didn't have people carrying paper or plastic bags either; everyone now carried reusable cloth bags for their shopping ever since cities and states began outlawing stores from using the kind that filled landfills for decades.

But crime still happened, and there was only so much the police could do. Especially when it was filled with underpaid and overextended men and women who often turned to less than savory activities themselves. Most weren't doing criminal things, but like

Williams and Vanzetti, they could throw their weight around and get what they could.

Jimmy looked for the things that the police overlooked, the things that people didn't report or call in.

"To your left, half a block up," came Wendell's voice in his ear. Wendell was getting better at his job, too, noticing things before Jimmy did. "The man in the red coat, he's trying to get money from that shop owner. I don't think he bought any fish from him though, bro. As a side note, the value of graphene just shot up, looks like you made almost a hundred grand in a few minutes. The T.A.L.O.N. Agency just acquired one of the small companies you invested in."

"Mhm," Jimmy mumbled, scratching his nose to cover the fact that he was speaking. He walked closer to the men, making it obvious that he was watching. The man in the red coat looked at Jimmy, said something to the other man, and then turned and walked away. "I can't just go tell him to give it back. The guy who owns the place would get in trouble and just get beat up for it later. "

"Duh, you think? Follow the guy, once he gets far enough away, then approach him."

"And do what? Beat him up? Don't you think he'd recognize me, the same way I can recognize other people?"

"We deleted your real accounts online, and gave you dummy accounts. They won't get you that way. But I guess you might get tagged from the police reports about your mom, or some traffic ticket some time. So, what do we do? I thought we were out here to stop crime."

"We?" Jimmy followed the man, despite his arguments against a confrontation. "I don't see us out here, only me. But I have an idea."

"You gonna use your whammy on him?"

"You'll see, and make a note to order a motorcycle face wrap thing for me. I'll also need headgear of some sort," Jimmy dropped his hand as the guy looked over his shoulder before ducking into an alley. "Ok, time to go to work."

Jimmy cleared the heads-up display on his glasses using the cardphone attached to his wrist, like a watch from the old days, then quickened his pace to get to the alley before the man disappeared. Seeing his target pacing while talking on the phone, Jimmy leaned against the mouth of the alley and squinted at his quarry. The thug stepped on a can, slipping and falling to the ground, cardphone flying into a puddle. It wouldn't be hurt, tech was too good at this point to have a little water hurt it. The man swore and climbed to his feet, kicking at the can. His other foot stepped on the shoelace that had come loose of the foot he was kicking with, and the man fell again, tripping himself without meaning to. Swearing louder, the man looked around and noticed Jimmy.

"What do you think you're looking at?" he yelled at Jimmy.

"Nothing," Jimmy shrugged. "I heard the racket, and thought someone might need some help."

"I don't need no help," the thug climbed to his feet, careful not to step on the shoelace.

Jimmy squinted again, and the man kicked at the can again. It flew away, rebounded off the wall and hit the man in the face with a popping noise, breaking his nose. Shouting more obscenities, the man stumbled around with both hands covering his face. He lurched backwards and hit his head on a low hanging fire escape. The man spun around lashing out at the metal ladder, and another crack sounded as he broke something in his hand.

Screaming, the man staggered away and stepped into the puddle where his phone had landed, crushing the device under his sneaker. It shot out from under him and he lost his footing. His head came down hard against the brick wall of the building and he laid still.

"That was awesome, buckaroo!" Wendell shouted through the beat of music, the theme of the old Spider-Man by Aerosmith. "Was that your voodoo at work?"

"I don't know, bro," Jimmy walked up to the man and tucked a card that said 'Bad luck follows those who take what is not theirs.' into the jacket pocket of the unconscious man, "maybe the guy just had some bad luck."

"Maybe it's just karma," Jimmy adjusted the motorcycle half-mask and ran his fingers through his short-cropped hair before putting on his helmet. The neoprene face wrap was double-sided, one side looked like a face with a handlebar moustache, and the other looked like a military-style, black breathing apparatus. There was a breathing filter in it, just in case. The helmet was light, but made of the strongest stuff Jimmy could buy.

"Maybe," Wendell said through the electronic link, "or maybe Bad Luck Jimmy has a secret weapon, and finally stopped beating himself up with it, and instead turned it on the bad guys. By the way, bro-ski, I programmed your prototype graphene wrap on the bike and helmet to switch from basic black to the copper-and-brass skin. Just punch the control on the panel."

"Thanks," Jimmy checked the rest of his gear. The gloves were charged, his digi-contacts pre-programmed for night vision, and his single lens, wrap-around glasses set up to zoom in as well as give him the usual info in the heads-up display.

A few other gadgets had joined the baton flashlight on his tactical belt, the pouches full of useful stuff. He was prepared for almost anything, and had practiced blindfolded to pull things out to help memorize where he had put it all. His hoodie had the dark blue side out, and he could reverse it for the reflective bright safety orange later. He hoped flipping the mask, jacket, and skin on the bike and helmet would be enough to make him blend in if he got in trouble, and not look like a vigilante.

The information about the gang that had been harassing people downtown was downloaded, including their usual routes. He would aim for one or two of them tonight, disrupting their activities, and maybe broken noses and hands would discourage a few. He knew it would only stir the wasp's nest in the long run, but if he could get them riled up, they would make mistakes and the police would have to notice. He even had a police tracker that sent the 'officer down' distress signal, and Williams and Vanzetti's contact codes ready to bring help once he had a few hoodlums on the run.

Twelve months after making his life-changing decision, he was on his way for his first real mission. His mother would be proud. She had always said he could be more than what he was. She always knew, but he hadn't. Now he did. And he was ready to show the world, from the shadows, that no one else would ever have to suffer the way he did when he lost the only person who ever believed in him. Genesis sang about the *Home By The Sea* as he flipped the switch and his bike hummed to life, and he was ready to go change his life again.

Travis I. Sivart

CASE 2143
CODENAME: ROYAL FLUSH

To Whom It May Concern at The T.A.L.O.N. Agency;

I am Johnny Rocket, P.R. agent to the rich and famous, and I am sending out this press release to clear my client's good name. When I am done telling you the facts, the press will no longer want to muddy the name of this honorable man, and all will be as clear as water.

My client knows he doesn't have the most awesome power around. In fact, he knows he is a second-rate hero at best. There were only a handful of heroes in existence at the time of Exposure and the Rising, including the gadgeteers, but he ranked close to the bottom of the super hero pool. He doesn't have a popular power like flying or being super strong. His only ability is to interact with water on a personal level. He can become water, move through water when he is in his liquid form, and can walk on water (which is one of the coolest things he could do). He can't shoot water from his hands, make water jump, explode, rain down, turn to ice or steam, or anything else useful.

He can't have a secret identity or wear a stylized costume, because clothes don't change with him when he becomes water. He can take a bullet and slow it down with his water body, but this leaves him naked. His mode of travel is through water pipes. It is a quick method of travel, but it means he often goes places via the sewer system. And that is how he got his name. He wishes it was because he could make playing cards come to life like the villain, Army in Wonderland. Or that he could make them explode like the inventive gadgeteer genius, Ace in the Hole and his side chip, erm, kick, Poke-Her Chip. Any of that would be cool, but that is not his fate. No, destiny has dealt him a much crueler hand, and the press called his bluff and named him. He is a high-profile celebrity and a child in the royal line of a high-ranking British Duchy. While he was attending the Emmy's the comet dusted the Earth with its scientific pixie dust and people with super powers started cropping up. This was the day his powers kicked in.

The award show was attacked in the middle of its live broadcast by The Venom, a half man, half snake villain that spat gooey greenish phlegm that made one nauseous for a couple days. Usually it made people vomit on contact, but that wasn't because of anything other than how disgusting it was to be spat upon by a naturalist, dreadlock-wearing hippie with the lower half of a snake, starting six inches below the hips. He was there that day to 'stick it to the man' and help 'tear down the establishment', and the celebrities were the perfect targets.

I would love to tell you that it was an epic battle and will go down in legend, but with all the news coverage that night, I don't think I can get away with it. Venom came in, hacking gooey loogies on people left and right, and Royal Flush melted into a puddle. But never being one to give up easily, he then swished around the floor towards the heinous serpentine villain, and was trampled into the carpet by the panicked crowd. It was then he found the strength under pressure to pull himself together, literally. There he stood, as naked as his enemy, but without the cool tail. To make things more embarrassing, it seems that the water he turned into had been cold and it showed when he was back in his human form. The press had snapped pictures left and right, documenting one more unimpressive attribute of poor Royal Flush.

At that moment, the door burst open, and in stepped the woman that would soon be my client's partner in more than one way. Spatulette was an exciting figure, and struck a pose in her black spandex body suit. As everyone knows from her publicity shots, she has wide hips and thick thighs and apparently her beanpole upper body was the handle of her namesake. She displayed her newly found powers like she had been using them for years, swatting Venom with the telekinetic construct that resembled a large kitchen spatula, then slid it under him with a gesture of her hand and flipped him into the air.

The man-snake writhed in the air and his tail shot out, grabbing the chandelier above the rows of seats. From that new position, he continued to rain down his goobers of ickiness. Spatulette tried to swat at him, but she had her limitations, and apparently sixty feet straight up or so was beyond them. That is when she saw the dripping wet, naked figure of my client, the soon-to-be named Royal Flush. She yelled at him to help her, and shoved a telekinetic spatula underneath him, and flung him at Venom. The man of liquid flew through the air with fluid grace, returning to his watery form. He enveloped the reptilian terrorist when he hit, covering the man's head and upper body with his own viscous mass. It was less than a minute before the snake-man plummeted to the seats below, unconscious. My client protected the criminal from any serious harm to his head during the fall, and then withdrew from the enemy, literally. Royal Flush was unharmed except for the half dozen football-sized dollops of noxious toxin floating in his watery physique. He squeezed the gooey gobs of green goo from his body as Spatulette sashayed up to him.

She took his hand into hers and smiled at the press as the cameras flared, lighting the room in a dazzling array of camera flashes. And that was the first photos of many with the two together, her with one fist planted on her wide hips, the other holding his hand, and his remaining hand covering his nudity from any more public exposure. Seconds later, he melted away, and the cameras followed his puddled path of purloined pride straight to the drain, where he made his escape from the attention. Spatulette remained behind for interviews, revealing her super-heroine persona to the world. My client was not so lucky, and so was named by the press. And that is how Royal Flush was made.

Needless to say, the royal house he belongs to has become quite the focus of the news for the few weeks after this incident. They decided to make the best of it and hired me. In the past eighteen months, Royal Flush has had quite the illustrious career. We have accepted only the most prestigious corporate sponsorships, including Speedo, Evian, and Carnival Cruise Lines. We have stayed away from the less savory suggestions, such as Tidy Bowl, Summer's Eve, and countless pool companies. Royal Flush cannot wear the logos due to his abilities, but appears in advertisements and public appearances, as per the contractual obligations, as well as making a pithy and clever sound bite mentioning a sponsor at each capture of a criminal.

It was about eight months ago when Spatulette finally caught up to Royal Flush again, during a trip to Atlantic City. Apparently, she had been posting on a certain online classified site, in their 'Missed Connections' section, hoping to catch his eye. During a photo shoot on the boardwalk, the notorious water monster OMG-zilla attacked in retaliation for his reptilian comrade's capture by my client. This was a much more difficult fight, but RF was in his element, literally. I must confess that Spatulette did more than her share of the battle, swatting, smacking, and shoving with her powerful ability. She ended the battle when she flipped a loaded panel truck carrying lumber into the beast's face. I guess you could say he should have 'saw' that one coming, but she 'nailed' him.

The whirlwind romance began shortly after that. I think that my client had been lonely in the public eye and wanted someone that understood what he was going through. Spatulette fit that bill. She is from a different world than my client, having been raised in the southern parts of the United States. She is outspoken and brash in contrast to his refined and cultured style. But they still get along well. I think he found her refreshing, and perhaps even a bit freeing. They go everywhere together. It seemed the world has seen its first Super romance!

The longer people are around each other, the more they see of the other's true self. Royal Flush soon realized Spatulette's deeper interest. She wants babies. A direct quote from Spatulette at a press conference is, "My name by definition means, 'having a broad, rounded end and a narrow accentuated base.' In other words, baby got back! And those are also known as 'good birthing hips'". She began accepting sponsorship from the likes of Huggies, Gerber, and Good Housekeeping. Not that anything was wrong with that, but it did send a clear message, especially when she agreed to take part of her contractual pay in diapers and baby food. The press ate it up. Of course, I mean the show she was putting on, not the baby food. She was going to make super babies. This is when my client realized that he was not of the same class and position to marry Spatulette and broke off their association. Also, his body is no longer like a normal person's body, so he can no longer be intimate or procreate the way normal people do. Their relationship was never consummated, to

Spatulette's frustration. From this information, you can see Royal Flush has broken off any association with Spatulette and nothing to do with this latest publicity spree that Spatulette has undertaken.

Sincerely,

Johnny Rocket

P.R. Agent to Royal Flush

Royal Flush circled the drain again, literally. Spiraling downward, he sought the quickest way to the latest destructive occurrence by his recently jilted compatriot and lover, Spatulette. Slushing through the drainage system of downtown L.A. was no easy task. It was a dry and arid land and it took a lot out of him. The hero drew upon the water in the air and pipes to replenish him as he traveled.

He had no idea what he would do against the hormonal rage of the ticking biological clock of a woman that could splash and spatter him the same way a kid in galoshes gleefully handles a puddle. Her powers had grown since they first met. When she first took the spotlight, her telekinetic constructs were barely visible and about the size of a manhole cover, but now she could change their color and shape, and they could be as large as a compact car. With the right leverage, she could overturn a fully loaded dump truck. His powers, in contrast, seemed to be growing in a trickle. He could barely maintain a humanoid form when liquid, and even that gave him a headache. He tried manipulating water and had managed to make the whirlpool in the bathtub swirl quicker, and drain the bath faster. Not very impressive. But something had to be done, and he knew this enemy better than anyone. He was raised to face any adversity, whether with diplomacy, tact, strategy, or as a last resort, force.

Royal Flush had found other abilities within his repertoire, such as seeing. It was not the way most people see, because he did not have eyes, organs, or even sensation like normal people. It was more of a moisture-based sonar combined with an inner peace that sent waves through him to describe his surroundings. In the beginning, he didn't even notice the difference, because it all came naturally. It was only later, when meditating in the gold-plated bucket (he couldn't use lesser metals, the salinity of his water form corroded them) that he had been given for such purposes that he realized his awareness could be expanded far beyond normal human sensory range. In fact, he was able to sense anywhere he could be connected to moisture, which was everywhere on the planet. This is how he rolled, in waves. And that is how he now tracked Spatulette.

The heroine-turned-rampaging villainess was currently zooming along one of the many super highways of the city in a jacked-up, four-by-four, pickup truck, flinging cars like hotcakes with her giant spatula. Feeling the need to stop her before she hurt anyone else, Royal Flush expanded his consciousness, taking it to the next level and moved it to where he sensed something. In this particular case, Spatulette.

The hero felt his body begin to coalesce on the highway, drawn together from the air, the moisture from car exhaust, and evaporated water from dozens of sources as small as the sweat off an ice cold bottle of soda. People smacked their lips together, experiencing dry mouth, and reached for their coffee or designer water only to find it empty and their thirst unsatisfied.

The diesel truck stood the height of two regular cars, barreling towards Royal Flush. He could see the look of recognition on his ex's face. Her shoulders were hunched and a look of deranged glee was in her eyes. The vehicle lurched forward when she slammed the accelerator to the floor. His body splattered against the grill and rained down on the hot asphalt with small sizzles, like water drops in a hot iron pan. A small whirlwind haze spun where the hero had stood a mere moment ago and sped up, his body reforming, unhurt. He faced the opposite direction, looking at the truck sliding to a sideways stop.

Spatulette's face twisted in rage, and she leapt from the truck, pulling her tight cutoff shorts from regions unmentionable. Her ribbed halter top rippled in the breeze, accentuating that she considered less clothing better than more.

"You're all washed up, boy," she growled.

"Oh my, not with the press level phrases again," he retorted with a dry air.

"Any man would be proud to be my beau, they all just flip for me, but not you. No, you're too good for the likes of a country girl like me!"

"Please stop. I would rather be crushed under your mad creations than suffer another attack of a play on words."

"Fine then, get ready to be flat as a pancake!" she screamed at him.

A sigh rippled along his body.

Taking a gunfighter's wide legged stance, the woman glared at her ex-lover. With a broad sweep of her arm she created a huge spatula, the size of a sheet of plywood and slammed it downward towards Royal Flush.

He was better prepared this time, though. Expanding his form, he grew three times his height in a split second, and reached upward to catch the weapon. But he did not.

It passed right through him and struck the ground hard enough to press into the scalding asphalt and form a rectangular depression three inches deep. Royal Flush swirled around, in a mist, expanding his limited form beyond corporeal bounds. The man-shaped cloud seemed to heave another sigh, and drew more liquid from the surrounding area.

A fog settled, obscuring Spatulette's vision but increasing Royal Flush's ability to 'see' a hundred times over. He could feel each breath and heartbeat of every person within a half mile. He could hear the tingles of electric in the power lines and car batteries.

Reveling in his awareness, a realization came over him: Mother Earth doesn't fight with direct attacks in most cases, but rather gentle sweeps that people call a force of nature. And that is what he was; a force of nature. He was not a man of liquid, no more than a rain cloud was only a cloud of rain. He was a complex system of countless interactions, and he could consciously orchestrate them.

He let his mind dance across his options, opening himself more than ever to his awareness.

Spatulette swatted blindly at him with her power, she was a like a rumble of thunder followed by a momentary spark of lightning inside his cloud.

He would have smiled at that analogy if he could smile in his current form, because it was then that his human creativity blended seamlessly with his nature, given awareness and a solution presented itself. Pulling in the fog bank he had become, he thickened it around the woman that had drawn him here and thinned it around the other people within his cloud. A lingering tendril danced across a power line, seeking the one minute gap that would allow him to call upon his own electricity.

Feeling the hum and vibration of the tainted man-made version of lightning, he channeled it within himself and collected a charge. His senses roamed across the woman that wanted nothing more than his babies, and he knew she only did as nature dictated, just as he did. He gently caressed her, and could taste her own electrical pulses dancing across his senses. He savored the sensation, connecting his own stored charge to her delicate quivering pulse, and released his own bolt of electric deep inside her. Her body quivered and quaked, her head fell back and her breath came in short gasps. He held her as her body shook, losing the ability to support itself and crumpling under his tender ministrations. He lowered her gently to the ground, her body still trembling, and withdrew from her, leaving only a mixture of her sweat and his own warm moisture coating her body.

The flashing lights of The T.A.L.O.N. Agency vehicles sprayed through his body as he drew himself back into a more human form. The agents rushed forward, rolling the villainess over and cuffing her hands behind her back.

Royal Flush withdrew, lost in his own awareness, realizing he was no longer like these creatures. He was much more expansive, but much less focused than these beings. He filled himself with more moisture and expanded, wafting upward and away from the gathering news-hounds and pressing questions.

To Whom It May Concern at the T.A.L.O.N. Agency;

I am Johnny Rocket, P.R. agent to the rich and famous, and I am sending out this press release to clear my client's good name. Once again I tell you my client, once he became a hero, could no longer biologically function as a normal man. Meaning he could not be responsible for this latest revelation.

After her detainment at the hands of my client and arrest by the authorities, Miss Spatulette had her day in court with a jury of her peers for the heinous deeds she committed and was sentenced accordingly. She has been imprisoned since that time. Earlier this week, when she revealed her delicate condition it was a surprise to us all. The doctors say she is three months along. That would be the date of conception right about the time of my client's last battle with her. He had not been with her in any romantic sense for months before that date.

Though we would like to verify this with Royal Flush, my client has not been seen since that fateful day in Los Angeles. His family is deeply concerned and misses him very much. We all continue to pray that he will return to us safely.

Sincerely,
Johnny Rocket
P.R. Agent to Royal Flush

CASE 307
CODENAME: STILL BORN

The wind blew through the open window, rippling the curtains, the screen making a flumping noise as it billowed in the gust.

Dan moved past it, his red sweater straining against his gut that preceded him. He juggled a plastic cup - whose color matched his sweater - and a paper plate with blue floral print around the edge filled with Swedish meatballs, cheese, crackers, and a few token vegetables smothered in Ranch dressing. He looked around the room, trying to find the least depressed or depressing person to talk to. Someone not boring, either. Taking in the crowd at the funeral, he looked over the slim pickings.

Gaynelle's, the deceased, children were in their fifties and performing their expected duties at an event such as this; her siblings were all well past seventy and stood in clumps of sympathetic friends commiserating about their own age and ailments; and the handful of small-town mourners were mingling with the others, offering condolences and eyeing the things around the house like sharks waiting for a beachside yard sale. Dan avoided the three men in dark suits, not wanting to deal with the stone-faced and coldly reassuring funeral home employees, and headed for a man dressed in a brown leather coat and khakis. He turned sideways to squeeze past Nancy and Judy, one woman comforting the other, and sidled up to Mikel.

"It's warm," Dan juggled his plate to get to the fork, unsuccessfully. He thrust his drink into Mikel's hand and stuffed a meatball into his mouth with his fingers, chewing with gusto and licking the sauce off his fingertips.

"Warm days agreed with Gaynelle, she always loved the sun. I remember sailing with her and David on days like this," Mikel spoke with an accent Dan couldn't quite pinpoint. The man glanced at the drink in his hand, set it on the windowsill, and wiped his hand on his pant leg. He rubbed his goatee with the other, and looked out the window before continuing. "Nothing like a thick jumper, a sea breeze, and open water. She loved that. She would giggle and squeal, like a young girl, leaning into the wind. David used to laugh at her, but you could see the love and adoration in his eyes."

"Dude," Dan said around a mouthful of food, "why would you mention her dead husband at her funeral?"

"This isn't a funeral," Mikel corrected, adjusting his jacket over the ivory turtleneck he wore, "this is a life celebration. No corpse lies in the room, or anywhere else in the house. I guarantee that."

"Well, don't tell those funeral home guys, or the family, they'd be pretty upset if they thought was some big joke."

"No, it's not a joke. This gathering today has a very real purpose. And those aren't funeral home employees in the suits; they are from The T.A.L.O.N. Agency and are here to witness to the final farewell of someone they invested a lot of time and money into, as they have watched everything she has done since they first found her. The T.A.L.O.N. Agency found out about her when she previously died, but not the first time she did so. People have seen Gaynelle's corpse on several occasions; the first time on the day she was born."

"Really?" Dan muttered with a mouthful of meatball, unsure which tidbit he should ask about first.

"Yes, she wasn't breathing when she was born. Came out colder than her mother's womb. Back then, it was a miracle they could revive her. A true miracle. And in her childhood, she was constantly sick. Had some issue with her white blood cell count. Gaynelle took the phrase 'life blood' more seriously than most."

"Why?" Dan stacked cheese on crackers, moving the broccoli and carrots out of the way, while only half listening to the foreign man, more enthralled by the exotic accent than the information Mikel offered.

"When she was young she had transfusions, was leeched, and they even tried dialysis once she was old enough, nothing seemed to fix it. Not until she died again. That was when The Agency took interest in her."

"She died again? What do you mean?"

"I don't know if this is the time or place to discuss it," Mikel peered across the room. His gaze took in Gaynelle's brother and two sisters, her son, daughter, a half dozen other guests, and the three men – who all stood in separate corners of the room – in matching black business suits, with identical Bluetooth earpieces in their ears, and watched them watch the room.

His eyes fell upon Mae, the meek woman who was Gaynelle's tenant and close friend the last few years of her life. The thin woman stood against the wall, shoulders folded in on herself, and eyes rimmed with red from crying. She wore a black summer dress with cream colored flowers on it, small bursts of red in the center of each bloom; it belonged in a decade long past. The woman had her hair pulled into a bun. She looked younger than she dressed, but Mikel knew her to be older than most would guess. Her eyes darted around the room and she wrung her hands. Slipping through the dining room doorway, she disappeared down the hall.

"Mikel," Dan said, a hand on the man's arm, "don't leave me hanging like that. You can't say something like that and then just leave it."

"Yes, I can. Leave it be. You just want juicy tidbits of gossip, and that isn't appropriate. This was a great woman who touched the lives of every person she came in contact with, whether they knew it or not. She may not have had headlines in the news, or been splashed around on the vids and TV, but she changed the world more than your limited scope could ever understand. People need to hear the good stories right now, not the tragedies."

Mikel turned away from Dan, who was left staring between the man and frowning at the vegetable-strewn plate in his hand. Mikel stopped for a moment to let Gaynelle's daughter, Donna, and another woman pass in front of him.

"She owned at least a dozen properties, all of them historical." Donna said to Judy, shrugging as they went into the kitchen to get another tray of vegetables. The graying woman set the tray down, turned and leaned on the counter. Her face showed more exhaustion than grief, "This one was once a hotel, built in the 1880s. It had been a brothel for a while, before they restored it in the 1950s."

"Why would they ever restore a whorehouse?" Judy wiped her hands on a dishtowel. "And why would your mother buy one?"

Donna shrugged and popped a cherry tomato into her mouth and chewed. She wasn't a pretty woman, but not homely, either. She was a bit squat, not thin like her mother had been. Her dishwater-brown hair was pulled back into a functional ponytail that disagreed with her semi-formal black dress.

"Mom was always eccentric. She liked things with a story to them. She loved telling a story, when she wasn't living one. She never wanted to stay home, even when she was raising her family. She would have dozens of magazines lying around showing different countries and places around the world. Once we kids were grown, she was off like a flash, running around the world and sending postcards. And when she met David, there was no stopping her. Even when he was sick they didn't stop. Did you know he died while they were away on one of their little adventures? I don't mean to be disrespectful, but I was almost glad when her husband died so she would finally settle down and let me take care of her. She was too old to be running around like she did."

"I thought she was a neat lady," Judy loaded the tray with more crackers and cheese. "I mean, she didn't fit in so well with this small town, but she was always happy. Even when she was complaining about something, she would make jokes. We would watch her waltz into the diner while we were all at the breakfast counter, full of life. She'd never sit with us women like she should have, though. She'd sit with the men, or off to one side with the, well, other people."

Donna shrugged again, her eyes misty as she finished loading the tray. This was the first emotion that Judy had seen from Gaynelle's daughter. Judy reached out and squeezed her arm.

"I'm sorry," Judy patted Donna's wrist. "Sometimes I don't think when I'm talking. Your mother's properties sound very valuable. How many did she have, and will you get any of them?"

"About eight or ten. I have to find out. I know they were all here in Virginia though, and every single one of them older than her. She had a penchant for old places. Here," Donna handed the older woman a full tray, "help carry this out."

The women passed through the dining room, the guests smiling sad smiles at Donna as they passed into the hallway. They passed her aunt and uncle, Mary and Earl, and continued to the front parlor.

"She was always small, but never frail. At least not in spirit." Earl lifted his bourbon to his lips and sipping at it before throwing the whole glass back. He exhaled harshly, licking at the drops in his unkempt moustache. He topped the delicate crystal rock tumbler off from a bottle on the windowsill. Holding the glass to the light and admiring it, he thought of how his departed sister never gave the proper respect to the finer things in life, like the expensive crystal glass, and used them every day instead of saving them for special occasions, like today.

"She was an odd one though," Mary moved her short veil away from her face to take a deep drink of the merlot wine she held. She glared at one of the dark-suited men as he looked into a bedroom off the wide hallway, then cross the hall to the bathroom. "Damned agents. I don't know why they are even here. I hope they don't think their agency is getting any of the stuff my sister left behind. That belongs to family, not strangers. I know they did a lot for her, but they shouldn't be here. It just ain't right. Remember when The T.A.L.O.N. Agency first showed up? We thought it was a blessing that they were willing to take the weight of the medical bills from our folks. Maybe even take Gaynelle away so we didn't have the burden of having to watch her."

"Yeah, but it did get weird," Earl said and drained his drink, ice clinking as he gave a breathy cough afterwards. "I mean, the first couple times it seemed fine. She'd be gone for a few weeks and come back all healthy and happy."

"Except when she committed suicide." Mary muttered, dropping her voice as her nephew, Larry, came from the parlor and passed them to go into the dining room for another drink. He was already listing, but that wasn't unusual for him. Larry liked his drink, and on an occasion like this, it was to be expected.

"When she was in her late thirties?" Earl asked, squinting.

"Yes, when they took her away for a month and kept her locked up for observation."

"I remember. There were a string of murders while she was

away. Creepy stuff. Charles Manson type stuff. Brutal killings, and people drained of blood."

"Earl! This isn't the place to mention such things!" Mary whispered at him, but leaned in closer to keep talking. "But I remember visiting her at The T.A.L.O.N. Agency medical research place, and they shooed me away because they needed to do a transfusion. And you know what?"

"What? Is this the story about that man?"

"Yes, and I swear it's true! One of the men who came in to give her a transfusion was one of the murderers. One of the six men they found dead."

"Well, that didn't have anything to do with her. She died again in that hospital, by her own hand they said. And they saved her again. Two weeks later she was out, and the murders were over for at least as long."

"And they did bring her in once a month for therapy, but she refused to stay overnight anymore. Said she didn't like their methods, and didn't trust them."

The man in the suit came out of the bathroom, finger on the wireless phone nub in his ear and the two fell quiet. They watched him look at them, into the dining room, then turn and head into the parlor, passing another one of the dark-suited men who was coming out. The two men nodded to each other as they passed.

The parlor was crowded and overflowing onto the veranda outside, which overlooked the road. The smell of cookies permeated the air, mixing with pungent perfumes and colognes. Mikel stood by a wingback chair and the fireplace, studying pictures in bright frames that stood out in the 1940's décor of the room. One wall was covered with dozens of crucifixes of different kinds. People sat on a wood trimmed divan underneath, chatting awkwardly and sipping at cans of soda and glasses of liquor. Mae stood just outside the door, her hands on her elbows in the cool breeze, glancing at the agent who had just entered the room from below her eyelashes.

Nancy stood a head taller than June, Gaynelle's other sister, and was pointing at the wall of religious symbols.

"Was Gaynelle Catholic?" Nancy wiped at a spill of wine on her grey sweater.

"No, not at all," June's mouth puckered, like she had a glass of lime juice instead of tonic water. "She just collected these, thought it was funny. I think it was disrespectful. But there was enough about my sister I didn't like. At least she's at rest now."

"Do you think so?" Mikel turned to join the conversation. The women looked at his smile, and both frowned.

"Yes," Nancy answered when June didn't. "Why wouldn't she be?"

"I always thought she was a bit of a free spirit," Mikel answered, "and I'd like to think she is just beginning a new adventure out of the reach of those that judged her or tried to use her."

"Well, I never!" June sputtered, and turned and stomped away. Nancy glared at the man's smile before sniffing and turning to follow June.

Mikel chuckled, looking around the room. Mae was making her way towards him, avoiding touching any of the other people she passed. She had her hands on the opposite elbows as she stopped in front of him.

"Did you know," Mae started, then faltered. "Did you know Gaynelle?"

"I knew her a while back, and one or two other times."

Mae's brow furrowed, trying to figure out what that meant.

"Oh," Mikel said, still smiling, "we didn't date or anything. We were just friends when I was in town. She was always up for an adventure. Whether that was a ride through the country, a trip to Europe, or anything in between. She is an exceptional woman."

"Yeah, she is." Mae smiled, and then her voice caught. "Was. She was an exceptional woman."

"I think she got very tired at the end before," Mikel hesitated this time. He studied the timid woman in front of him. "Before all of this. But now, she is free. Untethered. Things can be different now."

Mae nodded, but studied the stranger with a guarded look.

The last guest left, leaving Mae to clean up afterwards. She stood at the open door, watching the agent watch the last person get into their car and pull away from the curb. Mikel stood on the sidewalk, watching her. When she noticed, he turned and walked to The T.A.L.O.N. Agency car and leaned over to speak to the man inside. Strains of the conversation carried on the wind to Mae, but she couldn't understand what was being said. After a minute, the agent nodded, started the car, and pulled away.

Mikel looked back at Mae, and nodded with a smile. He turned and strolled away, hands in the pockets of his beige slacks. A whistled tune reached Mae's ears as she closed the door.

Looking around, Mae sighed at all the paper plates, plastic cups, wine glasses, and other various dishes littering the house. She was alone with her ghosts now. Gathering glasses, she walked them to the kitchen to put them next to the sink. She would have to hand wash them; this house had no dishwasher but her. Kneeling, she opened the cabinet under the sink and pulled a trash bag from the roll.

Wandering into the dining room, she began dropping paper plates and red plastic cups into the bag. Trays of half eaten food followed. She wouldn't eat it; she didn't like eating what others had touched. Each time she wandered past a window, she looked out, expecting to see the dark Agency car outside. It seemed whatever Mikel had said to the agent had brought a reprieve from being watched.

For now.

A tapping echoed.

Mae stopped and listened. It was a familiar rhythm, matching the bits of the song Mikel had been whistling. Mae followed the noise, and it got louder at the front coat closet. The woman set down the trash bag, and glanced at the front door to her right. Stepping forward, she opened the door, looking at the empty street. She looked up and down the road, but saw no one around.

The tapping continued from behind her.

Closing the door, she turned to the coat closet. Mae opened the door and peeked inside. Coats swung on the hangers from the door opening, three umbrellas leaned in the corner, and a variety of boots and shoes littered the floor. The tapping came from the back wall of the closet. Mae reached her arm in, hesitated for a moment, and then tapped on the back wall.

The tapping fell silent.

"Are they gone?" came a shrill, muffled voice from beyond the wall.

"Yes, they're gone," Mae giggled. "You can come out now!"

The wall opened away from the coats, revealing a room not much larger than the closet itself. On a bench sat a frail and wrinkled woman with gray hair to her shoulders and glasses with thin metal frames on her nose. A smile split her face when she saw Mae.

"Well, it's about damned time." Gaynelle's voice high-pitched and excited. "I thought they were going to stay all damned night. How long do they need to come in here, eat my food, sit on my furniture, and pretend to miss me?"

Gaynelle pushed through the coats, one hand held in front of her and bent almost in half so she wouldn't knock hangers down from the bar.

Mae gave her a hand, helping free the woman from her self-imposed tomb.

"Did all those damned agents leave?" Gaynelle straightened her pink sweater.

"Yes," Mae smiled from ear to ear at her friend, "Mikel chased them off before he left."

"Who? Oh, Jack. I know him as Jack, but he likes to use other names depending what's going on. Ok, let's go to the kitchen. I need something to eat, and then I need to go find me someone to eat so I can get back to being young and beautiful. I have several properties I need to visit, and don't worry, my kids don't even know these exist. But once we get there, I have jewelry you can sell so we have money, and then we can decide where in the world we want to go…"

Gaynelle chattered on as Mae made her a sandwich and they planned their next adventure.

CASE 1791
CODENAME: FEAR THE REAPER

Her parents screamed in the fire, She lay crumpled in the grass, leg twisted underneath her from where they had shoved her out the tiny second story bathroom window. She watched her daddy try to push her mommy out the same window, but only one arm, her head, and part of a shoulder would fit through. The woman cried in terror and pain, begging her daughter to look away and not to watch. The orange flames lit the chill autumn night as the six-year-old girl saw the large oak next to the house catch fire and embers began to rain down onto her broken body.

"Grannie, it's my birthday, and I am ten years old! I got two numbers in my years now! Come on, let's go try out my new kite!"

"Ok Lori, dear," Grannie rubbed her left arm, "I'm right behind you. Go on, I'll catch up.

Lorina ran into the field, leaping and giggling, her kite bumping along the fresh spring grass behind her. The wind caught the kite and it soared into the bright afternoon sky. The girl laughed and jumped up and down, turning her scarred face to the sun and closing her eyes and the string tugged and danced in her hand. She turned to call to her Grannie, and saw the older woman lying face down in the dewy grass, still clutching her left arm.

Lacey, her best friend, looked down, hair covering her face, as the three other girls circled Lorina and mocked her. They taunted her about the limp in her left leg, about the faded scars on her face, and how everyone around her died. They told her they were saving Lacey from dying, and Lorina would eventually make her die. Dozens of other kids stood in a circle in the school hall watching, as if in a trance, at the spectacle of the three most popular girls in school tormenting the misfit.

And the girl's only friend was torn from her by way of a social death.

The military gave her purpose, it gave her focus, and it gave her a place where she was accepted. At first, in basic training, she stayed apart from the others. She never joined the card games or social outings even after she was assigned. She knew she was different, and even if people acted like they didn't care about the scars, even if they didn't know about her history, they would all eventually leave her or hurt her. It was just the way things went. She signed up for infantry, and volunteered for missions. She would make a difference, even if it killed her.

Her commanding officers praised her courage and determination, but reprimanded her for not being a team player. "You're not the only one out there. You have to let others help, otherwise you're going to get them killed," were words she heard more than once. But she would still take the lead, against orders, and she came out ok. No one in her squad came back with more than minor injuries.

The day the other nine members of her squad cornered her outside the mess hall, shoving her into an alley between tents in the humid air of the South American jungle, was a day that she would never forget. Sergeant Mackenzie stood to one side, her back turned as Private Walters and Corporal Jenkins held her arms. The six others arrayed in front of her and stared her down.

"We've been in nineteen incursions together," Private Whitney, the book-smart kid, stepped in front of the others and looked Lorina in the eyes. "All of us. In all but three you have taken the lead. The first seven times you broke the command chain and took the lead, and the other nine you were given the lead because we knew you'd just take it anyway."

The others stood at parade rest, arms behind their backs and legs shoulder width apart, and nodded, giving silent support to the argument.

Lorina struggled against the hold of the two largest soldiers in her squad, who were being as gentle as they could in the situation. Jenkins twisted Lorina's left arm up behind her back, making the woman stand on her toes. her muscles and ligaments stretching and threatening to do more.

"Private Liddell," Whitney continued, "this will not happen again. You will allow each of us our chance at glory, and at danger. You can't protect us all, and you won't allow us to protect you. We like you. You are a machine out there, and right where we need you every time we go out. But we don't want to lose you, you're too valuable. To us. We need you."

Lorina quit struggling, a confused look on her face as the young man continued.

"So from this moment on; you will obey orders, you will join the squad fully, you will hang out with us, fight with us, talk to us, and be one of us. You will stop punishing yourself for whatever it is that happened in your past that you think you deserve to suffer for. You will have friends. That is an order, Private. Isn't that right, Sarge?"

"That's right," Mackenzie said, not turning around. "Now, baptize her and let's get on with this."

The five soldiers at parade rest stepped forward as Whitney stepped back. Their hands came from behind their backs, each holding a single champagne bottle and shaking it. The corks exploded, five staccato pops, and each hit her a fraction of a second before the alcoholic foam gushed across her. They upended the bottles over her head, Jenkins and Walters leaning away and loosening their grip to avoid most of the spray.

Lorina had been cornered, judged, and accepted, whether she wanted it or not.

Things were different after that. She had friends, nine people who cared for her, and she cared for them. She had a family again, something she hadn't had for more than a decade, something she had been missing for half of her life. That made it hurt even more when three weeks later, the bomb took out Jenkins, Mackenzie, and three others just before the machine gun fire tore through Walters and two others.

In a rage, Liddell took out the hidden tree nest with a grenade, taking fire as she tried to protect Whitney. She rained hell down on the men squatting in the underbrush with her rifle, and dissected their guerilla tactics with the surgeon's scalpel of her sidearm as the superior force was decimated by one woman who didn't have the lead that day.

Lorina watched the light go out of Whitney's eyes in the bed next to her in the infirmary. Everyone she loved died. And now she lay broken and alone.

Again.

She was death, and she brought that with her wherever she went.

"Hush," the therapist said, her well-rounded, middle-aged voice soothing, "it's ok. You're safe, no need to cry. You're safe, safe in bed here in the testing quarters at The T.A.L.O.N. Agency. What you saw was just a blend of dreams and memories, things your mind put together to create pain for you. The feel of someone leaving your life, forever."

The smell of a perfume that hinted at a blossoming flower blended with cinnamon from the doctor blended with the tart antiseptic smell of the medical supplies. The rubbery smell of petroleum jelly wafted through the room as Lorina Edith Liddell flinched under the leads attached to monitor her pulse, brainwaves, and other metabolic functions.

"That cannot happen anymore," Doctor Carroll leaned closer to her patient, her vinyl and metal office chair creaking. "You will never be left alone again, whether awake or in your dreams. But we need your help to make this happen. We need you to open the doors in your mind, so we can make sure you're never left alone again. Relax, it's ok. You were almost there. Practice your breathing. Deep breath in for seven seconds, hold it for four seconds, then release slowly over six seconds. Your fears can be controlled. They can be overcome.

"I will be watching over you. I will see you through this. I will protect you in the night when you feel the most alone. Open your mind for me now. You have to trust me, allow me inside, help me break down these walls you have built. And then we can begin to build a new world."

The doctor continued talking, droning on to relax her patient.

The eyes of the woman on the table went blank and her lids grew heavy, her head listing to one side.

The technicians in the next room captured the images in the patient's brain, translating the electromagnetic pulses into pictures, and changed them to be sent back and reprogram the soldier's perception of her current reality.

Sydney Roberts wondered what the patient was seeing when staring at him. The patient had a name, but he didn't like to think of them as people with names when he did these things to them. He was here to build the robots. He was here to protect the world.

He sent the nanites into the woman's blood stream, hoping the organic coating on them would allow her body to accept them rather than fighting them as foreign invadersThe would be fine, because he had programmed them himself. Just as her body would accept the subdermal graphene base sheets and the over armor that linked to them, it would accept the thousands upon thousands of microscopic robots that would control her body and brain chemistry, releasing adrenaline, dopamine, and others when needed. They would encode her genes on the fly, so she would heal at the optimum speed for her caloric intake, allow her to sleep less, and move faster. Sydney built the robots, then installed them.

The technician glanced across the screens monitoring the patient's vitals and programming downloads. On a side monitor he checked his bank accounts, triggering another transfer of cash. Part of it went into The T.A.L.O.N. Agency's account, and a small stipend slipped into his. He funded this department largely through his extracurricular accounting, and no one ever complained. Rival corporations fell because of internal embezzlement, and the T.A.L.O.N. Agency snatched up another corner of the markets.

This was what you had to do to save the world. It took a lot of money. To build these robots, to create an army. The airships, weapons, and other toys took time and money. Money and time.

Getting a foothold in every major city across the world wasn't cheap or easy. And it was all to make the world a better place. It wasn't easy to take over the world.

She should be ready by tomorrow morning, ten A.M.

"The vanillas are getting antsy, and lining up on each side of the issue," Lorina said.

"Don't call them that," Doctor Nora Pilcher said, avoiding the topic.

"They call the ABNs, deviants, or chimeras, depending which side of the issue they fall on. Chimera if they still believe in fairy tales, and want something wondrous to appear in this world. Deviants if they tend to believe in hell and brimstone, because it still sounds like a logical word with scientific backing, but is just a side step away from being a devil."

"They should be calling them Homo Minutus, or ABN at minimum," Pilcher leaned back in her chair. "Have you been able to access the computer system well enough without using a keyboard?"

"Yes, I'm scrolling through information right now. In fact, I am searching the terms we're discussing. Well, that I am discussing, and you are avoiding discussing. Why is that, Nora?" Lorina asked. When the doctor didn't answer, the soldier went on, "T.A.L.O.N. of course stands for Tactical Analysis Logistics Oligenetics Nanotechnologies Agency. ABN stands for Adjusted Bioengineered Normal, and is often referred to as a AB Normal, or Abbey Normal in the street slang. Homo Minutus ties directly into the Latin creed or motto of The T.A.L.O.N. Agency, Mutatis Mutandis, which means 'the necessary changes have been made'. Shouldn't that read that the necessary changes will be made?"

"You would have to ask the board of directors, Lorina. Can we please get back to our task? Are you experiencing any discomfort when accessing your abilities or using the computer interfacing?"

"I can't speak for what the board of directors intended, but I think they mean to justify what has already been done rather than announce what is to come. Following the philosophy of 'better to ask forgiveness, rather than permission'. At least that is what I seem to see when I search through their personal records."

"You shouldn't be in those."

"If I shouldn't be in them, then they shouldn't have given me the ability to get into them."

"They didn't. They set up safeguards and subroutines that to stop you from wanting to look into sensitive information which you shouldn't have access to."

"But they also gave me the capability of bypassing or overwriting harmful or intrusive cyber-catechisms."

"Lorina, that doesn't make sense. That applies to a religious doctrine, not the programming linking your mind to informational databases."

"Isn't that exactly what their ethical and moral blockades in my head were? Sometimes, we have to do more than just follow orders."

"That's dangerous talk. They designed you to contain these ABNs that have broken free of their contracts and stolen company secrets and hardware."

"Do you really believe that, Doctor Pilcher? Don't you know that these heroes existed long before The T.A.L.O.N. Agency? The Agency made more to either compete with them, or to control them. Just as they have done with every other sort of competitor they have ever run across."

"Does this make you a hero then, Agent Liddell?" the doctor scrolled along her laser keyboard, gazing at her screen.

"Perhaps I misspoke when I used that word, Doctor." Lorina said with a rueful smile. "Heroes don't exist. And if they did, I wouldn't be one. I am a weapon created to suit a purpose. I don't want glory, or to wear a costume. I also am not above doing what needs to be done when the time comes. All my training points to that. I am no hero. Heroes have a moral compass, and lines they won't cross. I lack those things."

"You may have a purpose, but you are much more than just a tool or a weapon, Lorina. You are still a person."

"Am I?" Lorina searched the windows and the skyline outside. She always seemed to be focused on something distant, using her peripheral vision to watch things near her. "Doctor, did you know there is a being here on Earth who is thousands of years old? Its name is Zagreb, and it's an asexual alien from a different dimension, or reality, or whatever. No one is sure. This is the oldest living ABN we know of in existence. He has been playing with genetic manipulation for millennia, and recently created OMG-zilla who attacked the Jersey Shore, and The Venom who fought with the British royal who became a force of nature, Royal Flush. The second oldest being - a vampire-like woman named Gaynelle Jacobson - was nearly a hundred years old before her recent death. A suspicious death, by the way, considering she should have been able to live for centuries more than she did. It is being called a suicide, but I am already finding correlations and patterns that may indicate that she faked her death. And of course, since I have come to that conclusion, The Agency has now launched a full investigation to determine if I am right. The benefits of the links in my head, I am never alone with my thoughts.

"But there are dozens of others, hundreds if you count the incidental reports that have no definite proof of powers or abilities and instead rely on hearsay and coincidence. They actually have people wearing costumes now. Ace in the Hole and his protégé, Poke-Her Chip, who use graphene playing cards laced with an electric pulse that explodes on contact have created an enemy who goes by Army in Wonderland by their creative outfitting and themed weapons. Wonderland can actually make the pictures from playing cards animate. No one is sure if it in in people's minds or if they are real, but the property damage left behind isn't an illusion.

"Some are simple people, like Jamie Erich. He's a conman who uses his blended telepathic-telekinetic abilities to make people think they have a ghost issue. Or James Earnest Weinbaum, better known on the streets as Bad Luck Jimmy, who started working out and learning to fight after his mother was killed in a mugging. These guys may be harmless, at least for now, but what about Hector Rodriguez who was one of our third-generation ABNs? He's out there and still has his abilities. They couldn't shut him down, now I get to hunt him. Or what about the ex-military man attacking a South American government with an army, even though he's blind? Is he a hero, or a crazy guy? Does he have any 'necessary changes'? Or the professional assassin that seems to be able to possess people in comas. He or she could be anywhere, we can't trace that one except after they finish a job. Or what about the ones we created through our own actions, like Vigil from Chicago? She got sick, and when it passed, she seemed to be stronger and more coordinated than ever before. But she didn't do anything with that ability, until we illegally kidnapped her son. Now she has gone off the radar, though we have an idea where she is now, because she is patrolling the streets to protect people. Do we take her out? If so, is it to protect people, or is it to gain her secrets?

"Did you know that conspiracy theorists think there was some sort of exposure to an agent that caused 'The Rising' of super heroes? Crazy, especially since we know that these beings have been around for a lot longer than anyone knows. But maybe there has been an influx recently. There is a point where certain people begin getting restless and seek more than just existing. This has happened before every renaissance and also before every social collapse. These people are the catalyst for failure or great advances.

"Does this bother you, Lorina?" Doctor Pilcher asked. "You have always wanted to serve a greater purpose, and not be alone. Now you have both. Shouldn't this be a good thing?"

"Sure, I guess it should be. But sometimes I want to be alone. Not all alone in the world, just alone in my room. Now I'll never be able to think something without it being recorded and tracked, analyzed and picked apart. Considered by philosophers or psychiatrists. Since not having any possibility of solitude, I realize how much I want to be alone sometimes."

"But being alone, with no one around is what drove you to extremes in the past. It caused you pain, fear, and anxiety. So did the thought of having others around you, you thought you brought them death. Now, you have someone with you all the time, and they cannot get hurt. Because we are connected to you through your thoughts. Had you just become used to being alone?"

"I don't know if I had become used to it, or if it is something people need, but when I say I need to be left alone, I need to be left alone. It lets me find my balance. It's a launching point, an emotional crouch to leap. Each time I do this, I get further along on the path I am searching on. Just because you aren't with me doesn't mean you can't be in danger. From the type of beings we are facing, there is no safe place. They can enter your mind, just like the Agency can, but one uses nanotechnology, the other uses something else. And we don't know exactly what that is, and it is my job to get those people so we can study them and learn how they do what they do. People won't be comfortable until they know how it is done."

"Why do you think that is, Lorina?"

"It is because of a fear that disappeared a long time ago. Humans are on the top of the food chain, and have been for thousands of years, and we are no longer hunted by anything. But, being hunted is our greatest fear. There is terror in being the target of something so much more powerful than yourself, that you're helpless to stop it. Or being road kill, and slain without any intent or purpose. And these ABNs represent something that can hunt us, or even kill us without knowing or caring they did so. And that scares the hell out of us. So, the Agency has made me, and others like me. And I will hunt down these ABNs, and bring them in. And whether I kill them in the field or not, I bring the end of their life to them."

"Ok Lorina, I think we had a good session, but our time is up now. I will schedule your next appointment with the receptionist and send you the e-confirmation, ok?"

Lorina sat up, blinking away the image of Doctor Pilcher from her head. The afterimage of the office windows and city skyline faded from her vision. The grey square room around her was home now. The upper half of one wall reflected the muted light of the indirect lighting in a mirror, and showed the alcove closet, and the small chest of drawers Lorina stored clothes in. The other corner showed a sink and toilet within a shower stall. Her nanites showed no one beyond the mirror in the observation room.

Sitting upright on her bed, she scanned through her email, finding the confirmation for her next therapy appointment. It usually happened right before her virus scan, but she had begun separating the two because of a sneaking suspicion of other information being removed during the weekly file cleanup.

Mentally flipping through the account, an email in her spam file caught her eye. The photo of the sender was a fit, middle-aged man with a square head, pearly white teeth, and a form fitting black t-shirt. But the name didn't match the photo. The message read like standard junk mail, but something about it drew Lorina's attention. Shutting down her electronic relays - imitating the virus scan function that would normally run at this time — she examined the letter in her mind.

From: Miss Melissa Nkem <victor@victory-fitness.com>
Reply-to: Melissa_Nkem02@yahoo.co.jp
Date: April 24, at 3:39 PM
Subject: Your Unpaid Fundss

Dear Friend,

I am Miss Melissa Nkem. A computer scientist with C.B.N. I am 26 years old, just started work with C.B.N. I came across your file which was marked X and your released disk painted RED, I took time to study it and found out that you have paid VIRTUALLY all fees and certificate but the fund has not been release to you.

The most annoying thing is that they cannot tell you the truth that on no account will they ever release the fund to you. Please this is like a Mafia setting in Nigeria; you may not understand it because you are not a Nigerian.

The only thing I will need to release this fund is a special HARD DISK we call it HD120 GIG. I will buy two of it, recopy your information, destroy the previous one, and punch the computer to reflect in your bank within 24 banking hours. I will clean up the tracer and destroy your file, after which I will run away from Nigeria to meet with you.

If you are interested. Do get in touch with me immediately, You should send to me your convenient tell/fax numbers for easy communications and also re confirm your banking details, so that there won't be any mistake. For phone conversation, please call me on +2348115354496.

Regards,
Miss Melissa Nkem

The email read like any scam, broken English and bad grammar littering the text, but something else niggled at Lorina. Debts paid, and funds not released tickled at her memory. It hinted of things said when she was in the military, but more than that shadowed it. There was a message here, one that spoke of conspiracy within The Agency. C.B.N. was close enough to A.B.N., it was only one letter changed, and that letter could represent the word 'changed' to replace 'adjusted'. The mention of wiping her disk after copying it, so only one copy remained sounded like freeing Lorina's mind from the

Agency's leash.

Lorina considered the possibilities. This could be a test and a trap from an enemy agent, or even the Agency itself. Or it could be a genuine offer of help. But Lorina didn't feel like she needed help, did she?

She studied the email again, wondering if she should follow up on it in private, or bring in the resources of the Agency as she hunted down the source.

"I'll worry about it tomorrow," she decided aloud, getting ready to go out on the hunt for ABNs. "You reap what you sow, and right now it is time for me to be The Reaper, and sow those who fear my coming."

The Reaper was on the hunt. Her target was Hunter Law, aka The Hawk, a man known by the Agency as someone who could detect ABNs and possibly even determine what sort of talents they had. Someone like this should be an easy collar, but then, he wasn't going to let it be easy. He had trained with mercenary and survivalist groups for more than two decades, as well as serving as a Navy Seal back in the twenty-teens, when the war in Iraq and Afghanistan was still the top news and the United States bickered about negligible things like a black president, which bathroom a person should be allowed to use, and if the world was actually experiencing a warming trend or not.

The Agency files showed the man had amazing hand-eye coordination; whether using a ball, a bow, a gun, a boomerang, a slingshot, or just throwing something - he didn't miss. Reaper mentally scrolled through the man's abilities one more time, hoping to glean some tidbit of information she had missed before. Her genetically heightened speed, strength, agility, endurance, and mental processing should make her more than a match for anyone. Add in her subdermal plating, wired reflexes, nanite hyper-cellular repair systems, auto-targeting optical implant, and other technological upgrades, and disabling a team of the world's best soldiers should be like taking candy from a baby.

But she didn't believe in taking chances. The Agency wanted Law alive, and Reaper would deliver him in that condition. Law, or The Hawk as he preferred to be known, was an ABN that could hunt other ABNs. That ability would be invaluable to the Agency.

ABNs were dangerous animals, and animal was the right term. Like a rabid beast, they didn't follow the natural laws that others did. They lived outside the constraints of society and thought that rules didn't apply to them. It was that sort of sense of entitlement that crippled the country in the late teens and early 2020s. But these ABNs were worse than anyone ever had been. Their abilities made them dangerous to the whole society, and they needed to be contained or eliminated. If society couldn't be protected, then it would fall apart.

The gentle voice in the back of Lorina's head reinforced the thoughts of protecting the whole against the individual. Like a soothing hum of a fan or air conditioner at night, or the sound of car tires on the road while on a long road trip, the people in her head comforted her as they reaffirmed her feelings.

Reaper moved across the rooftops of NewLA, a city designed and built in remembrance of Los Angeles after it was destroyed in the Disaster of '27. No building had escaped untouched, and the freeways, highways, and streets were damaged or blocked with debris and swaths of broken asphalt. Anything nature didn't damage were torn apart in the Six-Month Riots. Fourteen major corporations offered to rebuild it eighty miles east of its original location. Insurance companies, oil conglomerates, media moguls, and tech giants all took interest. The T.A.L.O.N. Agency had brokered the deal. It took less than a decade, but a new city stood and was named New Los Angeles, but had been nicknamed NewLA by the social media pundits.

Reaper sailed across the gaps between buildings using her magnetic boots to propel herself. Climbing with their help to the seventieth floor and above, she gained a view of the city. The Hawk had taken up residence here, making himself into a folk hero of sorts and damning the corporate control of the megacity. He had been captured on camera several times, stopping minor crimes or halting a fledgling riot. Riots had plagued the city as refugees still came here to claim their part of the city. The corporations had promised help to any existing resident of the destroyed LA, but many didn't go through the proper channels and claimed they were being cheated.

The transmission implant in Reaper's inner ear began to transmit data of activity in the city to her and her graphene contact lenses lit up, the infrared and information displays coming to life. She moved across the city and within a few hours she had located her quarry.

He was perched on a third-floor fire escape, fifty-four floors below her. Up here, the wind was fresh and didn't carry the smell of ozone associated with the electric car engines or the fetid aroma of the mass of people who lived and worked below. The moon was a crescent and would not provide much assistance to her target on this cloudy night.

Take him quick, we need him alive and well if he will be of any use to us. The voice said through her receiver. *Remember, he is trained and dangerous and will put up a fight. Use your tranq darts to start, the electro-stunner next, and follow him until he drops.*

Reaper ran through the plan in her head. It was a solid concept, but the voice continued, *Use necessary force on anyone who assisted the criminal, even deadly force is acceptable.*

Anyone who helped The Hawk was breaking the law and committing treason on a federal level. Incapacitating or even killing people who thought they were doing the right thing didn't sit well with Reaper though. Perhaps there was a way to avoid that. Maybe she could talk to The Hawk, convince him to join her cause.

We're reading levels of doubt, Reaper. The voice broke into her thoughts. *Don't hesitate, it will create opportunity for the target to take advantage of that and turn it against you. This man seeks to destroy what keeps this country together. I will begin the reinforcing sequence in you so you cannot be distracted from your objective.*

Reaper's mind filled with a white noise that held an underlying message of hunt and capture The Hawk. Her thoughts slid away, helping her focus on what needed to be done. She locked her magnetic grapple onto the side of the building and lowered herself twenty floors, detached it with a signal sent back up the line and it fell past her as she reeled it into the backpack spool on her lower back. She repeated the process, pausing on the fourteenth floor to make sure she hadn't been sighted.

Thirteen floors below, The Hawk stared directly at her. Their eyes met across the chasm between the buildings and Reaper's skin crawled. This man took her in with a glance and weighed and measured her. Her range finder showed he was still almost a hundred meters away. She was still too far to use her incapacitating weapons; she had to get closer.

The sounds of the street below her cut into the noise in her head and the doubts and thoughts from earlier once again crept into her mind. The voice from the control room assured her that she was not alone, and she was doing the right thing.

Reaper threw her arm forward and her monofilament grapple launched itself with a thought, down and outward, biting into the building above The Hawk as the anchor shot backward from her elbow into the wall behind her. Gripping the line with her gloves, they formed around it and she slid downward towards her quarry.

His hand blurred, metal disks flying upward towards the wire.

The line vibrated when the blades hit, but didn't split, her wire. She breathed a sigh of relief. She was sure she would survive the fall, already projecting how to twist to take the least amount of damage, but it could mean losing sight of her prey. She hit the wall, bending her knees to take the impact. The rear wire retracted its barbs and fell, allowing her to use it as a repelling line to close the distance between the two.

The Hawk took flight, leaping from the landing of the fire escape to a window ledge, to a drain pipe, to the ground below.

Reaper hooked the line into her forearm bracer and it retracted into its compartment and the second barbs released their grip on the wall. She took another path to the ground, jumping sideways to a neon marquee, then to an awning, and flipping to the ground. Looking for her target, the neon of the advertisement panels on the sides of buildings filled her vision. Her electronic contact tagged him, and using various traffic and other cameras, followed his movement, his form showed up as an outline even beyond the cars between him and her.

She launched herself across traffic, cars slowing at her approach as their sensors detected her, as well as The Agency's computers disabling engines and steering the vehicles to give her room to pursue.

Reaper was in her element: the hunt. It was only a matter of time before she overtook him. She knew this man intimately, having studied his file and history. She knew him from his preferred wingtip shoes to his brown-feathered hair. She could picture his dark beady eyes and large protruding nose.

He wasn't a handsome man, but he was striking, even though he wasn't even two meters tall. Reaper knew his training and exceptional skill with hand-eye coordination and any projectile weapon whether launched or thrown. The man was passable in hand-to-hand, knowing some martial arts, but nowhere near as skilled with his bare hands as if given the chance to throw or shoot a weapon.

Reaper also knew that The Hawk would seek high ground for better visual ability if given the opportunity. She didn't intend for him to be allowed any chance to gain advantage. She slid across the hood of a car, dropping her shoulder to the hood as a throwing knife flew past her and embedded itself into the windshield of the sporty silver Milestone. The interior lit up, the car automatically making the driver aware of the impact and contacting the insurance company for repairs.

Landing in a crouch between lanes of traffic, Reaper's hand came clear from her belt holding her tranquilizer dart gun. She launched herself into the air and onto a bus, bringing her target into her sights. The gun popped, the magnetic launcher shooting three darts at The Hawk.

The man showed preternatural awareness and skill, kicking a plastic water bottle into the air to intercept one dart, one of his throwing knives knocking the second from the air, and snatching the third from the air and swinging his body in a circle, to send the needle back towards Reaper.

Her enhanced agility allowed her to move past it without a second thought, but her mind boggled at a man catching a two centimeter dart moving over a hundred kilometers per hour and redirecting it. She wasn't even sure she could do that.

The Hawk took advantage of her distraction and disappeared around a corner.

Reaper took to her feet and pursued at her top speed, shooting past pedestrians that barely realized anything was going on besides someone running past them. The hum of engines covered the sound of Reaper's tranq gun, and the acrobatics and print were the only thing to draw people's eyes.

Turning the corner at top speed, Reaper leapt into the air again, grabbing a traffic signal post and pulling herself upward to gain a vantage point to find the fleeing criminal. She scanned the crowd on the street, and almost missed the blur coming towards her from behind. Spinning towards the movement, she threw herself backwards and off the traffic post that spanned across the inner-city traffic clogged street, grabbing The Hawk's ankle. Twisting it with practiced ease, she turned herself above him as the flew through the air.

They jerked. She flew past him, his grapple attaching to the same pole they just fell from pullin him out of her grip. He released and flew towards her form where she slid across the sidewalk. She rolled as Hawk landed, his foot sliding across the ground but his knee finding her throat.

Her contacts fed her new information. He was using T.A.L.O.N. Agency intel, a specific style of fighting meant to take down her and other agents with similar gear and skill level. He had a connection inside the Agency.

Before she could think any further, he followed through with a combination punch, a jab to her right cheek and an uppercut to the left jawline.

Spectators formed a semi-circle around them. The voice in her head urged her to take advantage and use them as shields, distractions, or even weapons. The people were obstructing justice and were eligible for the full extent of punishment by the law, including being physically engaged. The voice continued advising; making it clear that The Hawk would defend the crowd and be distracted from his offensive maneuvers against her. It bombarded her with images of civilians being shot or pummeled and the great rewards that would follow, how it would be justified and commended.

The imagery settled like a net over the crowd and the two became one as the gun in Reaper's hand fired, toppling the people closest to her onto her attacker. The mass of people broke and ran, and Reaper corralled them using wrist launched flares to direct their stampede towards her adversary. She saw The Hawk's surprised expression a moment before he was lost in the tide of people pushing him away.

Reaper leapt to her feet, dodging between people so she wouldn't lose her quarry. The crowd parted before her, trying to escape her punishment for the crimes, fear in their eyes as they ran.

The Hawk disappeared into a Multi-Cultural Central American restaurant, pushing through the glass door outlined by a stone archway.

Reaper followed into the bright orange and beige earth tones of the eatery. The smells of grilled beef and chicken mingled with the crisp sensory bite of fried corn tortillas.

People shouted at The Hawk – some in anger as he pushed past them, toppling a large tray covered with beans, rice, burritos, chimichangas, tamales, and cheese sauce, others in recognition of a vigilante who was a hero to some and a criminal to others – and then shied back as the sleek military-type operative slid past their table on silent feet.

The Reaper rounded the corner, dodging between walls into the kitchen, metal spatulas clanging against the flat grill and voices shouting in Spanish. The Hawk pushed servers towards her when she entered. The smell of grilled meat grew stronger, thick earthenware plates flying at her, crashing against the plastic walls and shattering when they hit the floor.

She ducked under and wove around the trajectories of the dishes, The Hawk's precise aim only disturbed by her heightened reflexes.

The Hawk disappeared through the dishroom and Reaper pursued. She slid on the wet floor, used the metal wall of the walk in cooler to rebound towards her prey, and followed him out the back door. The cool night air surrounded her, bringing the stench of rancid dumpster trash to assault her nose.

The Hawk bounded up the wall, using l'art du déplacement - the art of movement known as parkour in the late 1990's and early 2000's. He gripped small crevices with his fingers and his feet found purchase where no untrained person could.

The Reaper followed in a much less precise, and more general, manner propelling herself higher on the building.

Using a neon projector as ballast she found her way to the rooftop, following her target across the night sky.

He disappeared into a skylight of a warehouse.

She followed.

He bounded down crates and leapt across empty air until he reached the floor.

She followed, jumping directly down using the stacks of wooden and synthmetal crates to slow her fall, ricocheting her way down. Her hand landed on The Hawk's shoulder and he spun towards her.

"I know you," The Hawk said, "they are in your head. You don't think the way they do, but they have you on their leash. Let yourself hear your own thoughts, Lorina Edith Liddell. We need to run, Come with me. Don't be their puppet, their slave."

Her head whined with the interference of the metal and crates around her, breaking the contact The Agency had with her mind. She raised her hand to her face, wiping away blood from her nose as her, ears ringing, her head throbbing. Sharp pain bit into her shoulder blades and back, and she spun to face the T.A.L.O.N. Agents firing darts into her and The Hawk. The world spun and she fell deeper into the rabbit hole.

Lorina's awareness swam into perception. She was strapped to a table, the cold metal under her, and the sharp smell of antiseptic in her nose. Turning her head as much as the straps allowed showed The Hawk restrained on a table next to her. She heard voices in a fog.

"Did the experiment fail?" asked a grey form to her left.

"No, we just have to go deeper into her head before she will give up her control."

ACKNOWLEDGMENTS

Here's to the many who inspired characters in this book; the brothers Raul and Geraldo Ayala who own and operate Los Portales in Tappahannock, VA and their employees Diego and Carlos; Hector and Paula Rodriguez who owned and operated Hogshead Cigar Lounge in Fredericksburg, VA and their customers and employee, Kim, Tawana, and Alfredo; and to the man who makes art that lasts as long as I live in the form of tattoos, Eddie Gonzales. Also, a quick shout out for Dawn Olsen, my Canadian friend who enjoys the same odd sense of humor as myself.

This wouldn't be complete without mentioning my weekly superhero gaming group who plays in this world; Andrea D'Amico who host our game on her channel (twitch.tv/AndreaLeChat), Elizabeth Pasieczny of Pickleman Productions, Daniel Carter of ItsWoodPodcast.com, and John Millington of Conquest Comics. Lastly, a raised glass to toast Bob Lowell, who has improved our lives and days with cannolis, boobs, and inappropriate comments.

My gratitude to everyone who inspires me in small and large ways.

ABOUT THE AUTHOR

Travis I. Sivart writes Steampunk, Social DIY, Science Fiction, Medieval Fantasy, Young Adult, Speculative Fiction, Horror, and more. Travis's writing style has been described as true storytelling, with the feel of sitting next to a fireplace and listening to a tale. He is also a father, public speaker, cook, pipe smoker, cat & squirrel lover, and so much more. You can find Travis on Amazon, Barnes and Noble, Books-A-Million, and other fine literary retailers, or at his website at TravisISivart.com or TalkOfTheTavern.com hosting his internet talk show, Talk of the Tavern (Sarcasm, wit, and a pub-like atmosphere),

If you enjoyed this book…

Please let others know by reviewing it on Amazon or Goodreads, and let others know your thoughts!

Other books by Travis I. Sivart

<u>Aetheric Elements: The Rise of a Steampunk Reality</u>
Automatons and airships, bustles and beasts, corsets and curses, dandies and dastardly deeds, all await you as you explore the cultures which evolved into a Steampunk industrial civilization. An anthology of nineteen tales of terror, mystery, and adventure.

<u>Steampunk For Simpletons: A Fun Primer For Folks Who Aren't Sure What Steampunk Is All About</u>
A primer followed by a guided tour through the world of steampunk, from the basics such as where to go and what to do, to the aesthetic of the arts within steampunk.

<u>27 Thoughts on Enjoying Life</u>
Twenty seven thoughts on helping create happiness in your personal life, success in your professional life, and even manage depression on a daily basis by suggesting ways to improve and maintain your mental, physical, and emotional well-being.

<u>Journal of a Stranger</u>
The thoughts, ideas, philosophies, and inspirations of a time traveling adventurer. Delving into the psychology of man, life's eternal questions, burning passions, and the quirky pseudo-science of his mind, and more.

<u>The Downfall: Harbinger</u>
The Talisman came again, but this time it didn't leave. The magical emanations of the comet have brought terrors from the bowels of the earth and increased the powers of an insane necromancer. The chaos above brought out others seeking to wrest control of the land. Five people from different walks of life are thrown together by these events with the knowledge that the world as they know it is ending.

9 781954 214408